# KINSEY'S DEFIANCE

## MADELINE MARTIN

*July 1341*
*Castleton, Scotland*

Kinsey Fletcher never cared much for market days. They were loud, crowded and filled with Englishmen trying to stir up trouble.

Like the two bleary-eyed sods pointing at them as Kinsey and her older sister, Clara, walked by.

"Ignore them," Clara said gently. "They mean us no harm."

"They would if given a chance." Kinsey narrowed her eyes at the men, who grinned salaciously in return. The arrogant fools.

"Ye can't go around picking a fight with every man who looks at ye." Clara led them away from the carpenter's stall they'd been perusing, and through the crowded streets. "Ye'd never get any rest."

Kinsey scoffed. "I'm not the only one they're looking at." Though sisters, their vastly different appearances went beyond their personalities to their hair, with Clara's being dark and silky straight while Kinsey's curls were bright red. Regardless, they both seemed to draw a significant amount of notice.

Not that it was anything Kinsey couldn't handle. Indeed, it was the exact reason she insisted on bringing her bow and a quiver of arrows to the market.

"Come, we're nearly done." Clara lifted the basket from Kinsey and examined the contents. They needed only a few nails and a bit of wool, and then they could finally return to their stone manor on the outskirts of the village.

It wasn't only Scots who lived in the village, but English as well, given that they were so close to the border between the countries, where the two nationalities tended to blend. How could they not when the lands were stolen by either country, then taken back, only to be stolen again?

But reivers often spilled over from England in greater numbers on market days. Some seeking items from the traveling merchants; others in retaliation for some raid against them, which had been a retaliation for another prior raid. On and on it went.

One day, someone would need to put a stop to it. And Kinsey wouldn't mind being that someone.

Regardless, the men all somehow wound up at the tavern with too much ale sloshing about in their heads and a keen determination to woo whatever lass they came upon.

Kinsey and her sister stopped at the blacksmith's booth, where Clara bent to inspect a bin of nails. It was a rare sunny day, one she would prefer to spend at home rather than at the market. The sun beat down overhead, and the dry, dusty air rose around them, mingling the fetid scent of too many people with the various sweet and savory scents of cooking food.

"They're all straight, miss." The blacksmith folded his arms over his broad chest. His gaze wandered appreciatively over Clara's slender pale hand, then up her arm and to her face.

"Ye always do quality workmanship, I know," Clara rushed to

reassure him. She lifted her focus to him, and her cheeks colored with a blush as she took note of his attention.

Kinsey shifted from one foot to the other in agitation. This was why they were always getting into trouble during market days. Clara was the type who wouldn't ignore anyone speaking to her. Not the vendors, who she politely declined when she passed, nor the men who approached her to compliment her. Clara would flush prettily, a genuine response she could never stifle, while offering a "Nay, thank ye," which was far too sweet to be taken as an actual rejection.

It only made the men press harder, and then Kinsey would have to step in to demonstrate the power of true discouragement. Usually with her bow and arrow.

It wasn't Clara's fault, of course. She was a beauty, though she never believed it regardless of how many men tripped over their hanging tongues as she passed. It was more than her wide, pale blue eyes and the full mouth they'd all inherited from their mum.

There was an innocence to Clara, a demeanor of genuine kindness. Mayhap that was why her good sister attracted the worst men.

Kinsey wasn't as oblivious when it came to men's notice. She knew they watched her as much as they did her sister. But she didn't blush at their flattery. She sliced them with the blade of her tongue and set them back a few paces.

The two Englishmen were still there, pointing at her now. One caught her notice and gave a cheeky wave with the tips of his plump fingers. Kinsey practically growled her irritation.

"Do ye think these will be enough?" Clara asked.

Kinsey distractedly examined the twenty or so pointed nails in her sister's cupped hand.

Kinsey nodded, though she had no idea how many were needed. Their eldest sister, Faye, had always been the one to attend the village on market days. Not only did she enjoy the task of shopping, but she also managed to procure the best deals.

Except now, Faye was married, living in the Highlands with a bairn on the way. And there was nothing for it but to attend the market in her stead.

Clara paid for the nails and thanked the blacksmith, who gave a slow, besotted smile as he accepted the coins.

They had only a length of wool to purchase, and then they could leave. Kinsey's shoulders didn't relax though, not with those men nearby. She glanced about and realized she'd lost them. Mayhap that meant they'd given up and—

"You're a pretty one." One of the two Englishmen stepped from the surrounding crowd and approached Clara.

A delicate shade of pink blossomed over her cheeks, damn her.

"Thank ye." Clara shyly ducked her head.

Kinsey didn't bother to hide her huff of aggravation. Clara would eventually get them both killed.

"I bet you're far sweeter than any honey I could buy here." The man stepped closer, swaying a bit. His friend stood behind him, saying nothing as he offered them a smile that looked ready to slide off his homely face.

Clara shook her head, her smile wavering with uncertainty. "Nay, I—"

Kinsey moved to stand before her. "She's not interested."

The man didn't bother to hide his lust as his gaze slithered down Kinsey's body. "And I bet you've got the right amount of spice to offset that sweet, eh, Red?"

She resisted the urge to cross her arms over her chest to shield herself from his foul stare. Not only would she not give him the satisfaction of knowing he'd unsettled her, but she also wanted to ensure she could draw her bow quickly.

"I'm also not interested." She notched her chin a little higher. "We'd like ye to leave."

"What if I want to stay?" He licked his lips.

She slung her bow off her back, drew an arrow and sent one

into the dirt just before his feet where he stood several paces away. He stepped back, and a second arrow landed where his other foot had been.

"The next one goes a little higher." She nocked another arrow, aimed it at his groin and smiled. "Is that enough spice for ye?"

"Kinsey." Clara's voice held a note of warning.

Kinsey could already hear the admonishment. Though, with Clara, it was more a careful reminder than a chastisement. "Remember what the constable said—the next time ye bring out yer bow, ye'll be fined."

But Kinsey wouldn't be fined. The constable made the threat often enough for her to know it held no weight. Then again, she'd only ever shot the ground. Would the constable continue to be as forgiving if she actually put her arrow into someone?

Eventually, she just might find out.

Today would not be that day, for the Englishman and his friend scowled and staggered away, grumbling their curses.

The cloth merchant was at the end of a line of booths, beside a cart offering jars of honey.

"Do ye need any assistance?" A voice asked from behind Kinsey.

From an Englishman to a Scotsman. God, how she hated market days.

"Commendable timing." She glanced over her shoulder.

The man was lean and tall, his brown hair neatly combed to the side, his high cheekbones evident with the hint of a smile on his lips. He was the most handsome man Kinsey had ever laid eyes on.

And he knew it.

What was worse, he was undoubtedly a nobleman. His clothes were too costly to be a reiver. Or even a merchant from the border for that matter.

Before she could open her mouth to offer a smart retort to

send him off, Clara spoke up. "Nay but thank ye for offering to help."

Kinsey gave her sister a long-suffering look, which Clara met with a patient tilt of her head. How was it she never got riled?

"Then mayhap ye can help me," the man said.

But Kinsey was already turning away, pulling Clara toward the cloth merchant who would undoubtedly take far too much of their time.

"Can we get the wool next week?" Kinsey asked under her breath.

"I'm almost finished with the new dress I'm making for Mum." Clara navigated the crowd of people as they walked. "I need only this last bit for it to be complete."

Her older sister slowed just before they reached the cart laden with bolts of colorful fabrics, the scent of dye sharp from the fabric, which had been warming in the sun. "I know ye don't like market days, and aye, the people can be...coarse, but Kinsey, I worry about ye. The constable said—"

"Excuse me, miss." The handsome stranger appeared at Kinsey's side once more. He smiled at her in a way she was sure other women found charming.

To her, it made him look like a false apothecary, selling off a bottle of common loch water as a cure-all potion.

Still, whatever he had to say would at least be more interesting than yet another discussion about the constable and his flimsy threats. She nodded to Clara to go on without her. After all, the vendor was only a few paces away. She would be able to keep watch on her sister from where she stood.

Clara hesitated, but Kinsey waved her on, and she finally made her way to the cart. The man was still smiling when Kinsey returned her gaze to him.

"I'm Sir William MacLeod," he said as if he thought the familiarity of his name would warm her to him.

It didn't.

"Ye caught my eye," he continued. "I had to come talk to ye."

And here it went...

Kinsey sighed.

"Ye're an exceptional archer."

His compliment took her aback.

"I beg yer pardon?" A glance confirmed Clara was at the cloth merchant and being left alone.

"I saw how confidently ye fired those shots." He nodded the way men do when they're impressed. "Ye're damn good."

Heat touched her face. "Thank ye," she replied.

Was she really blushing and thanking him? She was getting as bad as Clara. But then, no man had complimented Kinsey's skills with a bow before.

"I have need of a good archer," he replied. "How would ye like to join my men and me in the fight against England?" He looked over his shoulder to indicate a group of men outside the inn before returning his attention to her. "To rise with the return of King David and reclaim the land that the English have stolen?"

Her blood charged in her veins at his words.

She'd heard of King David's return to Scotland after his exile in France. He'd been there so long that she couldn't remember a time when he had been on Scottish soil. She'd also heard of his determination to take back what belonged to them.

And she could be part of that army.

How long had she wished to exact vengeance on the English for their betrayal of her and her family after their English father was slain in combat? How often had she lain awake in the manor, craving something more out of their quiet life?

This would be the ideal opportunity. The decision ought to be easy.

She glanced to where Clara sifted through several bolts of fabric with a careful hand.

Could Kinsey leave her family? Especially with their brother,

7

Drake, already working for an earl on the wrong side of the border, and Faye being so far away?

Indecision raged within her.

For how could she not fight for Scotland after so many injustices?

❦

WILLIAM MACLEOD HAD SPIED THE FIERY LASS FROM ACROSS the market. What man had not?

Hair like fire, ice-blue eyes that sparkled with a challenge, high firm breasts...aye, he'd have noticed her anywhere. But then she'd brought out that bow, quick as a snake's strike, and expertly pinned the arrows into the ground right before the Englishman's feet.

That was the kind of archer William needed under his command.

A bonny lass to warm his bed would be an added benefit.

And yet she appeared hesitant.

"If ye join my men and me in our efforts to regain Scottish land from England, I'll, of course, pay ye." He winked at her.

She frowned slightly, almost appearing as though she found his charm off-putting. Strange.

Her pretty lips pursed with shrewdness. "If ye pay me to do the job of a man, I'll take the wage of one."

There was something in the way she spoke that made her sound English. The Scottish burr was there, aye, but her words were less lyrical, crisper. He'd bet his life that she had mixed blood running through her veins, which meant neither country had likely been kind to her. He could use that to his advantage.

He considered what she'd said. While most men might balk at such a brazen demand, William found the logic of her request sound. "Consider it done. The pay of a man for the work of a man."

"And I want armor." She glanced behind him, where his men stood in their chainmail.

"Of course."

Her eyes narrowed with a look of cautious intensity. "How do I know I can trust ye?"

He studied her, taking in the blue linen kirtle hugging her well-curved frame. The garment was quality enough, but not grand. Certainly, it was absent fraying hems or worn spots. Which meant she was not poor, but nor was she rich.

Her bow and arrow were of better quality, mayhap the best he'd seen on the borderlands.

She wasn't unfounded in her lack of trust, especially on the border between England and Scotland, where treachery was prevalent, and reivers left everyone on edge.

She flicked her attention to where her attractive dark-haired companion pulled a bolt of fabric from a stack and handed it to the merchant with a generous smile.

William was running out of time.

"My father is Laird of Dunscaith Castle on the Isle of Skye." He indicated his family crest on the hilt of his blade, the bull's head expertly carved into the gold.

"And ye're his heir?" The weight of her assessment settled over him.

William squared his shoulders. "Why would I no' be?"

In his father's eyes, there was one primary reason—disappointment. It had started early on when William was a lad. The knowledge that nothing he ever did was good enough to satisfy his father.

After a time, William gave up trying.

He'd also stopped caring. Or so he told himself. But with his father now threatening to name someone else as his heir for the lairdship, William had no choice. He had to fight for his birthright.

This was his one opportunity to prove his worth by assisting

King David in reclaiming Scottish land. And William would stop at nothing to ensure he succeeded.

"I must go." The lass said abruptly.

"Can I no' get an answer from ye?" he pressed. "What's yer name?"

She smirked. "If I decide to join ye, I'll give it then."

"We leave at the first light of dawn tomorrow." A sense of urgency always helped spur prompt decisions. "Meet us by the inn."

Except she didn't take the bait. She lifted a shoulder with a maddening air of indifference. "I may be there. I may not."

She began to turn away, and he knew she would be lost if he didn't press his cause.

"Have ye or yer loved ones no' ever suffered at the hands of the English?" he asked.

She slowly looked back at him, and he knew his gut had been right.

"Ye've no idea," she ground out.

"Then why let them win?" He stepped toward her. Her eyes sparked in a way that told him he'd struck a chord, one he could readily play.

There was a sweet, powdery scent about her. Markedly feminine. He could envision himself gliding his lips over the hollow of her naked collarbone, breathing her in.

"The English have had their way with Scotland for too long," he said. "Starvation. Raids. Homes burned. Lives stolen." He shook his head. "No more." His hand balled into a fist. "King David will reclaim Scotland, and I'll be there. My men will be there. Will ye?"

Her breath quickened, evident by the swell of those alluring breasts against the neckline of her simple gown. "Dawn?"

He nodded, and she said nothing more, leaving to rejoin the dark-haired woman. Though she hadn't committed to accompanying them, she would be there.

Or at least he hoped.

Hiding a smile, he put his back to her despite the temptation to watch her depart and returned to the inn.

All his men had gone inside the sagging structure, except the largest warrior who merely lifted his brows at William's arrival. "Will she join us?" Reid asked.

William shrugged and tried to pass it off as though she were of little concern. "She says she'll think about it."

"That's as close to a nay as ye've ever had from a lass." Reid pulled his auburn hair back into a thong, away from his sharp-featured face. "What do ye think?"

"She'll show."

Reid smirked. "An early dawn departure, then?"

It was a tactic William had employed before. A highly effective one.

William simply winked. "Did ye secure the rooms for us?"

"Do ye even have to ask?"

William threw his arm around his second-in-command. There was a reason he'd asked his boyhood friend to be his right-hand man in going up against the English. Reid was resourceful, with a knack of accomplishing any task.

They entered the inn together for a bit of hot food and a few ales before settling in for an early night. As William ate and drank with his men, however, he couldn't stop his mind from wandering back to the bonny redhead who spoke with a blended accent. She was lovely to look at, aye, but many lasses were.

If her archery skills were as good as she'd exhibited, she would be invaluable as a warrior. They were in an age where a capable bow could give them an advantage, plucking off enough of the enemy to change the tide of battle.

She could be the pivotable point that helped him impress his father.

William hated the twinge in his chest at the thought of his da.

He shouldn't crave the man's approval the way he did, not when it had not been given in so long. But mayhap now...

He knew the night would be a fitful one as dawn slowly approached, with him wondering if the lass would join them or not. And he hoped to God that she would.

Kinsey was quiet on the long walk back to the manor, lost in the back and forth sway of her thoughts.

In one moment, she was determined to join the knight in his quest to vanquish the English, followed by a second later, when she decided it was best to stay with Mum and Clara. This was followed by yet another entreaty by her imagination of her shining in glory with her bow held aloft in victory.

"Kinsey," Clara spoke her name with emphatic patience, as though it was not the first time she'd done so. "What did the man ye were speaking with want?"

It was asked with such innocence that Kinsey immediately determined it would be best to remain in Castleton where she could protect her softhearted sister.

Kinsey's answer caught on her tongue, leaving her uncertain of how to respond. It wasn't that she couldn't lie, but that she'd never been able to with Clara. Her sister's faith in Kinsey made the false truths far too heavy on her conscience.

But while good-natured and gentle, Clara was also exceptionally keen, which made situations like the one Kinsey had landed herself in rather difficult.

Her hesitant reply was noted, evidenced by how the skin around Clara's eyes tightened. "What is it, Kinsey? Has something happened?"

"Nay," Kinsey replied.

*Just the opportunity for vengeance.*

"What did the man want?" Clara pressed.

"My expertise in archery," Kinsey said at last. Not a lie.

Clara's face blossomed into a smile. "How very flattering that he noticed yer extraordinary skill with the bow. Now I understand why ye didn't try to shoot him."

Kinsey scoffed. "Ye act as though I go about threatening every man in the village."

Clara didn't respond.

Kinsey shot her sister a look, but Clara was waving toward the house where their mother was bent over a row of beans in the garden positioned to the side of their home. Mum straightened as they approached, the bucket at her side laden with various vegetables.

She pushed through the garden gate and approached her daughters with a wide smile. "I trust it went well at the market." Her stare became decidedly pointed as she regarding Kinsey. "Any fines?"

Clara took the basket and gave Kinsey a sympathetic smile before slipping into the house.

Kinsey regarded her mother without a lick of guilt. "I told ye, the constable will never give me one. And I don't like how the men treat Clara."

"Ye're too fiery for yer own good, lass." Mum sighed and ruffled Kinsey's hair.

Ordinarily, the affectionate gesture was welcome. Except that now, suddenly, it made Kinsey feel like a child.

Aye, she was the youngest of the four siblings, but she had recently celebrated her nineteenth summer. And now, she had been asked to be a part of a rebellion against England as an archer. A warrior in the king's army and a woman whose pay would equal that of a man.

She wasn't a child.

Her mother seemed to sense the shift in her and smoothed her hair. "Ye're a good lass, though, my Kinsey girl. Always looking out for others."

Her words lifted at the reservations in Kinsey's mind and scattered them like chaff on a stiff wind.

"Aye," Kinsey said slowly. "'Tis a good thing to stand up for others."

"Of course it is," Mum said. "I'm proud of how ye always consider others. Especially as ye know, yer sister is so verra gentle."

Kinsey nodded, but it wasn't Clara on her mind. It was the people of Scotland: the men, women and children who didn't have the means to defend themselves against England's cruelty.

But she could.

In fact, she would.

Her decision had been made.

At that moment, the day took a profound shift in her eyes. The vegetables she helped her mother harvest through the afternoon would be the last she ever plucked from the small patch of land beside their home. The bustle of preparing supper with her mother quietly singing would be the last time she would smell her mother's savory cooking or sway to the lilt of her voice. Sitting around the table once the food was prepared as she laughed and ate with her family—this too would be her last.

She warred with the decision to tell them of her plan, and finally, when they were clearing away the remains of their meal from the broad wooden table, she broached the topic. "I heard gossip at the market that King David is planning to take back the land the English stole from Scotland."

Clara pursed her lips. Though she didn't speak, Kinsey could see she was puzzling over how she had not overheard such news as well. Especially when Kinsey had a conversation without her.

"And on goes the bloodshed." Mum frowned as she scrubbed a handful of sand in the pot to clean out the remaining bits of food.

"Don't ye think we should have the land back?" Kinsey asked.

Her mother set the pot aside with a heavy hand. "No' at the expense of the lives such an endeavor will cost."

Any argument Kinsey might have had to counter her mother's statement was nipped away by a pinch of guilt. Her mother was speaking of Kinsey's da, of course. A brave English knight who had died in battle. Their love had been the truest form, one that could not be severed even by death.

And so it was that Kinsey's mother lived with a broken heart. One she claimed to be worth the pain, thanks to the memories she carried with her every day.

Kinsey couldn't remember her da. Nor could she recall how the English villagers had shunned them afterward for Mum being Scottish. She did, however, have scars from the cruelty of the English as she'd grown. Not only the ones that scored her heart from their disdain and refusal to help but also a slight scar on her brow where she'd once been hit by a rock. The cut had bled ferociously as head wounds did, and she forever wore that mark of their hatred.

Mayhap that was why she fought so hard to defend others. For no one that day had come to her aid.

After her mother's reply, Kinsey didn't say another word about Sir William or her intent to join his men in their mission to take back Scotland's land. But nor was her decision swayed.

That night, when she bade her mother goodnight, she tried to burn every detail into her memory. How the skin of her mother's cheek was so petal-soft when they hugged, the love shining in her eyes, the soothing sound of her voice that had comforted as much as it had cajoled for the better part of Kinsey's childhood.

Clara hesitated to get into her own bed in the room she and

Kinsey shared after their mother left. Her gaze settled on Kinsey, sharp with a knowing perception. "I will always love ye, no matter what ye do."

It was as though Clara could see into Kinsey's thoughts and pluck out her decision to slip away before dawn broke.

Shame burned hot in Kinsey's cheeks. "I'll always love ye too, Clara." She hesitated before adding. "And I hope ye'll always care for Mum."

Clara's mouth tucked downward, but she nodded slowly. "And I hope ye'll always have a care for yerself."

Kinsey slid her a confident smile, appreciating the unspoken conversation running between their words. It wasn't a proper farewell, but it was enough to allay the ache coiling in her chest.

She allowed herself only a bit of sleep, waking every few moments with anxious anticipation. When the fire in the hearth was little more than embers, she rose from her bed to obtain the small travel bag she'd stashed away once she'd made up her mind.

Prior to leaving, she paused to write a short note. She'd composed it in her head while waiting for sleep, but scratching out the words onto parchment made them feel stilted and awkward. After all, how thorough was a farewell when it wasn't done in person?

She assured her mother she would be safe but offered no details. Knowing her family, Drake would no doubt come after her and Kinsey couldn't stomach the idea of him tracking her down to drag her off from the other warriors like a naughty bairn.

Once the missive was written, Kinsey took one last look around the house where she'd spent some of the happier years of her adult life. The two-story stone house had offered protection. Inside those sturdy walls, there had been no threat of attack, no hunger gnawing at their stomachs. There had been only joy and security.

And now, she would be leaving it all behind.

Shadows blanketed the interior, but she didn't need light to know where the table was that they'd shared their meals, the chairs by the hearth, where they passed many a night with stories and laughter. Aye, the home had always been filled with love.

She made her peace with her choice to leave, to fight, then turned her back on everything that had been so familiar for a chance to make right the wrongs of the world.

WILLIAM LEANED AGAINST THE WALL OF THE INN AS THE EARLY gray light of a new day glowed on the horizon.

"Any sign of her?" Reid took a position at William's right, leaning his back against the rough-hewn wall and crossing his arms over his chest.

William shot him a long look, which earned him a smirk from his friend. Silence fell between them as they waited, giving way to the sounds of dawn with the clicks of insects and chirps of rousing birds.

The air was wet and heavy with the promise of an impending storm. They would do well to begin their travel before the rain began.

Reid's hazel eyes were fixed in the foggy distance where the sun would soon start its slow ascent. "Is she bringing the dark-haired lass with her?"

"We dinna need her." William pushed his elbow against his friend's arm. "Did ye fancy her?"

Reid lifted a shoulder. "She was bonny."

William slid a glance at his friend. Reid didn't bother with women generally. They fawned over him, aye, drawn to his quiet, brooding demeanor. But he was never one to accept their bold offers. Reid's life had not been an easy one. His parents had been slain by the English when he was a lad, their home burned. He'd been orphaned and left to the mercy of others until the church had taken him in to care for him. Mayhap that was why he would rather offer lasses aid than bedsport.

In fact, Reid's comment about the woman from the market was the first William had ever heard him make.

"Mayhap we can ask after her once the archer arrives?" William suggested.

Reid shook his head as if the matter need not be bothered with. But it made William regret not having asked the archer after the other lass. Of course, he could discreetly discuss it with her once she arrived.

Unlike Reid, William was well aware of his impact on women and enjoyed its effects. Why not use it to his advantage?

A figure showed on the horizon.

Was it her?

William's heart jolted with hope. He pushed off the wall for a better look, squinting into the semi-darkness for the telltale sign of those luscious red curls.

"Well?" Reid asked. "Is it her?"

The figure was slender with a narrow waist, wearing a kirtle as evidenced by the outline of her body—a woman.

Victory surged through William. A proficient archer would offer the support they needed to succeed.

This woman was the final piece he needed for a successful campaign.

As she drew closer, she adjusted something on her shoulder —a bow.

Aye, it was her.

William grinned. "I told ye she'd come."

"Is that why ye've got a wee bit of sweat on yer brow, then?"

William ignored Reid's comment but passed a hand quickly over his forehead before approaching the lass. She strode toward him with determination, her face set with purpose, her hair catching the predawn light like fire.

His pulse ran hot.

God, what a woman.

"Ye'll join us then?" He gave her his most charming smile.

Once more, she did not appear impacted. Instead, she gave a single nod, her expression serious. "Aye. I will."

"We're pleased to have ye." He held out his hand in offering, intending to take her fingers and kiss the backs with a knight's gallantness.

She shook his hand with a firm grip. "The pay of a man for the work of one, aye?"

"As agreed."

Her gaze flicked behind him to where Reid still leisurely leaned his body against the main wall of the inn.

"Do I have the pleasure of learning yer name now?" William asked. "So that I can introduce ye to the others."

She narrowed her eyes, as though still skeptical. "Kinsey."

It was a strong name, fitting for a woman of such spirit.

"Well met, my lady." William offered her a little bow.

Women usually enjoyed a knight calling them his lady. Kinsey, however, merely looked at him without emotion. No giggle. No smile. Not even a hint of color to her fair cheeks.

"I'm not a lady." She tilted her head, a note of confidence to her demeanor. "I'm an archer."

"That ye are," he replied. "And we're fortunate to have ye."

He waved over Reid, who approached at an unhurried pace.

"This is Reid, my second-in-command." William indicated Kinsey. "And this is our new archer, Kinsey."

Reid nodded his head in acknowledgement of the introduction. Was it just William's imagination, or did Kinsey's cheeks flush slightly?

He set the thought from his mind. No woman had ever come between him and Reid, nor would one now.

William's men began to arrive in front of the inn with their horses strapped with packs for the upcoming journey into

England. He set about introducing her to the men, rattling off the names of the fifty guards and tenants his father had allotted.

Fib, the youngest of the lot at just fourteen, immediately planted himself at Kinsey's side, chattering on about their plans to aid King David and how things in the group worked. William let him carry on. After all, William would get a chance to speak with Kinsey more. The lad couldn't talk forever.

As it happened, young Fib might very well talk forever.

He didn't stop through their journey from Scotland into England or even when they arrived at their camp. The location had been selected as it was near enough to Mabrick Castle to easily spy on its defenses while the caves nearby still offered the ability to remain unseen in the thick woods.

Mabrick Castle, once owned by the MacLeods and stolen by the English. Surely reclaiming part of the MacLeod legacy would put William in his father's good graces.

Fib leapt down from his horse and shook the brown hair from his eyes as he unbuckled his pack. "That's how the pig came to live at home with my mum," he said, finishing a story he'd clearly been telling Kinsey.

"Like a dog." She laughed, her blue eyes sparkling with delight.

"Aye, just like a dog." Fib pulled his pack from his horse.

William stopped his horse beside them and dismounted. "Fib, is this how ye treat a lady?"

Fib froze with his pack lifted in midair and blinked his dark eyes before glancing at Kinsey. "Ehm..."

"Assist her from her horse and help her with her bags." William offered his hand to Kinsey to take.

She ignored his hand and leapt down, her feet landing soundlessly on the forest floor. "I'm being paid the part of a man, and I'll be treated as such. Unless ye mean to help every one of yer men from their horses and with their packs..." She cocked a brow.

William caught Reid watching her from several yards away

and didn't miss the chuckle he tried to hide. Nor did he miss the way Kinsey's gaze lingered on Reid.

*Damn it.*

William considered her, not entirely certain how to handle this woman who seemed to have her own set of rules. "If that's what ye prefer."

She gave a firm nod. "Fib told me everything to expect, such as training at dawn and how we'll keep watch before attacking the castle."

"Is there anything I can do for ye?" He let the question hang like temptation between them. "Anything at all."

Her eyes narrowed somewhat, then widened innocently as she bit her bottom lip. His gaze slipped to her mouth, appreciating how full and rosy it was.

Ah, yes. This was the reaction he was used to. He leaned closer. "Ye dinna need to be shy with me, lass."

"I confess," she replied slowly. "I'm curious about...someone."

She would be his by the time the sun sank on the horizon. The light, sweet scent of her teased at his awareness, catching the sweetness of her light scent.

His groin stirred with anticipation. "Aye?"

She looked up at him and blinked her long-lashed eyes. "Someone I find very appealing..."

It would be easy to tuck their bedroll away from others. He wouldn't want this beauty fast and in the dark. Nay, he'd want to strip her down and run his hands over her skin and get lost in her glorious hair. "Aye?"

She put a hand to the side of her mouth and her lips curled around the half-whispered name. "Reid."

**≈ 3 ≈**

**K**insey almost laughed out loud as Sir William's face reflected first his confusion, then his surprise. In truth, she wanted nothing to do with any of the men in the small army she'd joined. But she knew asking after Reid would discourage their leader's obvious interest in her.

Hopefully.

He glanced back at Reid, and Kinsey's stomach sank to realize the other man had been watching them as well. She might have just swapped one man's interest for another.

"I see." Sir William's eyes squinted slightly, his expression unreadable. "I want ye to go to the tavern with me."

Kinsey swung her gaze back to him, incredulous. Had she not just tried to dissuade his affections?

A smile hovered on his lips, making him look impossibly handsome. Which he no doubt knew.

"We need to gather information on the castle we'll be attacking," he said. "I assumed since ye sound so English, ye might be helpful to have with us."

So he hadn't meant it with romantic intent. And no doubt he'd intended her to be confused about the invitation. She smirked, refusing to allow him to see his ploy had worked. "Aye, of course."

"Once we've set up camp, we'll venture into the village." He gathered his horse's reins.

"I'll be ready."

He winked and strode away, leading his horse with him. She glanced at him as he passed with his easy, confident gait. His shoulders were broad, his waist tapered and hips narrow. He'd pushed up the sleeves of his leine past his elbows, and his forearms were bare, lined with muscle, evidence of his strength.

Damn him. He *was* attractive. More so than she wanted to admit.

She turned quickly away lest any of his men tell him she was staring. But not before noting that the man had a nice, firm arse.

*Damn him.*

She gritted her teeth and pulled her bag from her horse. There wasn't much to it. Two clean kirtles and linens, a comb, some tools to make more arrows and a bit of food.

"Do ye need help with that?" There was a slight crack in the voice, a hint of adolescence, and she knew immediately that it was Fib.

She glanced over her shoulder to find the lad grinning at her. He'd been kind on the journey, explaining with eagerness the routine the men had established, how they trained, what she ought to expect. He was an orphan whose parents had been killed by the English. His grandmother had raised him but died of a deep cough three years prior.

Kinsey had only lost her da, but she still recognized the lad's deep need for companionship. It was something she understood, something that resonated in her soul.

"Don't ye go trying to coddle me now." She grinned at him and tossed her bag over her shoulder before leading her steed to the cave where the men were all tethering their horses. The beast Sir William had provided her with was healthy and well-cared for with a glossy chestnut coat. "I can handle myself well enough."

Fib laughed, his throat flexing in his long, skinny neck. "Ach, I well know it. But I thought I'd try to be chivalrous."

"Like a knight," she teased.

His eyes sparkled. "Aye. Exactly like that."

"My brother wants to be a knight." Kinsey smiled to think of Drake, the oldest of the four of them. "I've never known someone more chivalrous."

Fib fell into step at her side. "What makes him that way?"

Kinsey thought on it as she led her horse into the cave where a trough of food and water had been placed. "He puts others first, trying to protect them no matter what." The way he had with them, ensuring they had shelter, enough food, clothing—even when he had nothing. "And he does what is right."

"Always?"

It was Kinsey's turn to laugh. "Aye. Always. It can be terribly annoying."

"How long do ye think until he becomes a knight?"

Kinsey lifted a shoulder. "He needs the right opportunity."

But that wasn't true. Yet another byproduct of English hatred. They would never accept Drake with his Scottish blood and the slight burr of his accent. Yet still, he worked for them, acting as Captain of the Guard for an English earl, one Kinsey had never met and did not care to.

She hated his need to work for them, to degrade himself for the sake of his family to keep them in such accommodating living conditions. Once she was making her own money, fighting as a warrior for Scotland, she would be able to help support Mum and Clara.

"I hope he is knighted," Fib said earnestly. "It sounds as though he truly deserves it."

"Aye." Kinsey switched the topic to horses rather than discuss Drake's futile hopes any longer. If Fib noticed the abrupt transition, he didn't complain as he proudly shared how he'd trained his own mare since she was a foal.

He stayed with Kinsey while they brushed down their horses and tethered them in the cave. Once done, they carried their bags to another cave where they were all going to sleep on bedrolls by the fire.

Sir William approached them with a pack, which he handed to Kinsey. "Eat something while the horses rest, then we'll ride to the tavern at sunset."

She peered into the bag and found enough bread and cheese for her and Fib as well as a wineskin of ale.

"Can I come?" Fib asked, his eyes lighting up.

Sir William ruffled the lad's already unkempt hair. "No' this time. Mayhap the next, aye?"

Fib's eagerness dimmed, but he nodded obligingly.

"Ye can tell Kinsey what we'll need her to do," Sir William said.

That brought a smile back to Fib's face, and he spent the rest of the time until the sun sank in the sky telling Kinsey how she would need to act inconspicuous at the tavern and what to listen for.

When she joined Sir William, Reid and a stocky man named Duff, Fib stood on the outskirts of their camp and watched as they departed.

"I hope he's no' bothering ye." Sir William nodded back to camp as they rode off, indicating Fib.

"Nay." Kinsey glanced back at the solitary figure in the middle of the forest. "He's eager to join ye."

Sir William's handsome mouth pulled down in a frown. "He's too young to be here."

Kinsey didn't disagree. "Then why is he here?"

"I couldna keep him from coming." He rode his horse confidently, his body gliding with a comfortable grace on the massive destrier. "I can, however, keep him from danger."

Kinsey suddenly regretted leaving her bow at camp. "Is there danger at the tavern?"

"He's a lad."

"And there's always danger where there are Englishmen," Reid added, to which Duff grunted his assent.

Kinsey put a hand to her belt to ensure her dagger was in place. Her fingertips met the braided leather wrapped around the hilt of her blade.

She couldn't throw daggers like Clara, but if left to defend herself, she would make sure she walked away alive.

WILLIAM FOLLOWED DUFF TO THE TAVERN. THE MAN HAD ridden ahead earlier that day to find it while they set up camp and rested their horses.

No doubt they'd be able to glean some information before spying on the castle the next day. Anything would be beneficial.

Bringing Kinsey, however, had been a risk. William knew that. But part of him thought the crisp English edge to her Scottish accent might put more people at ease. That and, if he was being completely honest with himself, he wanted to witness the interaction between Kinsey and Reid.

Not that he ought to give it a second thought.

If she was interested in his closest friend, so be it. However, he couldn't shake the suspicion that she wasn't being truthful. It wasn't arrogance that made him question her, but a feeling in his gut.

Mayhap her claim about Reid was simply to put off William.

But surely that couldn't be the case.

They entered a small village, no larger than the one where he'd found Kinsey and meandered toward the large, whitewashed building with a thatch roof and a picture of a mug of ale on a swinging wooden sign. Inside, there was the usual sight of reivers and travelers alike, swigging from mugs and flirting with serving wenches. The air was hot and stank of tallow candles, fatty meat stew and too many people.

If Kinsey was nervous, she hid it well beneath the confident tilt of her chin. There was a cockiness to it as if she were daring anyone to challenge her. It gave him pause as he questioned once more if bringing her had been a good idea.

A buxom blonde turned from a table, nearly running into William's chest. She blinked up at him, fluttering her lashes. "Can I help you with something?"

He indicated the group of them as they sat at an empty table. "Ales if ye please."

"Ahhh, a Scotsman." She sucked her teeth. "I like how brawny you Scots are. You know how to please a lady."

William chuckled in reply. Were it any ordinary night, he'd indulge her flirtation and let it carry them on to see exactly how much she enjoyed the company of a Scotsman. But this was no ordinary night. Not only because he had a woman with him, but because that lass was Kinsey, whose beauty was so fiery and bright, all others dimmed in her presence.

Which, of course, meant she'd attracted her own fair share of attention. Several men were openly staring; one hadn't even bothered to blink as he gaped at her, open-mouthed. The serving lass returned with another woman at her side, this one brunette, who beamed at William as they set the heavy mugs to the table.

After the two left, William and his party, pretending to be mercenaries seeking a paying job, kept their conversation light to ensure any of them could stop speaking and listen to those around them at any time. Thus far, nothing had been said about Mabrick Castle. But William wasn't discouraged. With the castle so close, there was bound to be gossip.

What he did notice, however, was how one man, in particular, stared at Kinsey. He was large with dark, neatly trimmed hair, like a soldier, his square jaw set.

Eventually, Duff left the table as planned, in search of whatever else he might find. The brunette wench returned to the table with her sights set on Reid. And while the man never took advantage of affection offered his way, he was never one to turn down the opportunity for information. As he let the woman lead him away, William couldn't stop his gaze from gliding over to Kinsey. Her expression remained blank with disinterest.

Even when they were all speaking, she had paid him little mind.

If she really were interested in him, wouldn't she have glared at the woman or tried to turn Reid's head with suggestive conversation when they were at the table?

"'Tis just the two of us." William lifted his mug. "Sorry about Reid."

The corner of her lips quirked upward. "Nay, ye're not."

He grinned. "No' entirely."

She rolled her eyes, though the action was absent any malice. "Don't ye have enough women fawning over ye?"

It had been his resolve to set aside any discussion of a relationship with Kinsey after their talk earlier—at least for a bit. But since she'd brought it up...

"There's someone else I'm keen on." He lifted his brows slightly.

She didn't press him, however. Instead, she simply replied with a light hum and drank her ale. A bit of moisture clung to her bottom lip, and she licked it off with a careless flick of her tongue.

His blood went hot.

God's teeth, but the woman was so damn attractive.

A man strode into the tavern and made his way to the table just behind William. "I'll need a hearty ale tonight after what we've been told," he said to his companion. "We're being sent to bloody Scotland."

"For how long?" Another voice asked.

Kinsey's eyebrow quirked up, and William knew she'd heard it too. He reached across the table and took her hand in his, as lovers would. She flinched and tried to pull her hand back, but he gave a slight shake of his head and discreetly indicated the men behind him with his eyes.

"Until their imposter of a king is defeated," the man replied.

William stroked his thumb over the back of Kinsey's hand. It was an act, but one he played willingly. Her skin was like silk beneath his touch, save for her fingertips, which were callused from her bow. Her eyes were a brilliant, pale blue. Stunning.

A tender smile played over her lips as she gazed back at him.

It was a bit stiff to be truly convincing, but it would do.

"What about the castle?" The man behind him asked.

His companion scoffed. "You know how things are at Mabrick."

Kinsey stiffened somewhat at the name of the castle. Her lips moved without sound, repeating the same, and her brow furrowed like she was searching her memory.

"'Tis too hot in here," she said.

Before William could ask what was wrong, she'd already stood up, pulling her hand from his, and walked out the door of the tavern.

## 4

insey's heart slammed in her chest. Mabrick Castle. She knew that name. It was the castle nearest Werrick Castle, where Drake worked as Captain of the Guard. She pushed through the heavy tavern door into the cool night air. Even absent the thick odors inside, she still found it hard to breathe. She needed a moment with her thoughts.

A middle-aged man with a hairline that had receded halfway over his pate approached her with a swagger. "I saw you when you came in."

Kinsey put up her hand. "Nay."

He stopped and frowned.

She had to get away, to think. How could she attack a castle so near Drake? What if he'd been sent to help and she shot him by mistake?

The man turned away, and she went in the opposite direction, slipping into a narrow alley in the hopes of losing herself in the shadows. Piles of refuse littered the sides of the building amid muddy puddles and a fetid sourness hung in the air.

"Kinsey."

The erratic pounding of her heart stilled. Sir William had followed her out.

A large, warm hand wrapped around her arm. "Kinsey."

She spun around at the familiar voice. Not William. She stared up at her older brother. "Drake."

"What are ye doing here?" The heavy shadows cast over his face and made him appear ferocious. "Who is that man ye're with?"

Suddenly Kinsey felt foolish to admit what she'd done. How she'd left Clara and their Mum to take back land from the English, especially when Drake's money came from them. The money that afforded them a safe manor and ensured they were well cared for. And now she was fighting against all of that, siding with her passions rather than her family's best interest.

"I...I..." she stammered.

His brow crinkled. "It must be bad if Kinsey Fletcher is at a loss for words."

She gave him a disparaging look.

"Did ye run off with him?"

She scoffed. "I'm no fool to lose my head over a man. Especially not one so arrogant."

"Are ye in trouble then?" Drake asked, his tone serious. He had more of a Scottish burr to his speech than any of them. Whether through being older when they spent time in Scotland when they were younger, or from all his time with Scottish reivers prior to working for Lord Werrick. And it always became thicker still when he was irked.

She shook her head. "I left home."

"Why?"

*To rise against men like the one who employs ye and has kept us all safe.*

She bit the inside of her cheek, unable to bring herself to speak the truth.

"Kinsey," he said in a warning tone. It was one he hadn't used on her since she was a child.

He never scolded her. He didn't have to. After all, it was never his wrath she dreaded, but his disappointment.

"I've joined the Scottish rebellion." There. She'd said it. Her gaze settled warily on his face to gauge his reaction.

His jaw clenched. "I would discourage ye from doing this."

"'Tis already done."

"Ye know I work for an English earl." His stare bored into her.

She wanted to look away, to block the force of his emotions. He'd never been one to say what was on his mind, but it was always there in his eyes. Right now, there was anger, aye—a rare emotion, but there regardless. But there was also discontent, and there was fear.

She nodded slowly.

He gritted his teeth as if in pain. "And ye know if ye attack Werrick Castle, I'd have to fight ye."

She swallowed and nodded again.

"This is foolish, Kinsey." He rubbed the back of his neck, finally breaking his burning eye contact with her. "The English know ye're coming. They're preparing for Scottish attacks."

"We're well trained." Kinsey didn't let her confidence falter. Not for one moment.

"Dinna tell me where ye're going or what ye're doing." He put a hand up as though to silence her. "I dinna want to know, so I canna be asked for it or forced to lie for ye." His lips pressed in a thin line as he considered her. "Kinsey…"

"I won't change my mind," she said stubbornly.

He shook his head. "I know ye too well to assume ye would."

The way he said it made her want to look at her shoes and toe the dirt. Though she kept her head upright, her voice was soft when she finally spoke. "I'm sorry."

"Stay away from Werrick Castle, aye? I canna…"

He couldn't battle against her.

"I know." She couldn't fight him either.

"And stay away from Mabrick Castle," he said in a low tone.

Unsure of what to say, she didn't speak at all.

His hand clenched into a fist. "I shouldna be telling ye this…" Indecision warred on this face. He was quiet so long thereafter that she thought he wouldn't tell her after all.

Indeed, something in her stomach told her she didn't want to know.

"The king has lent the castle a *pot-de-fer*." He glanced about, as though fearing they might be overheard despite his low whisper. "'Tis a large tube stuffed with black powder that can fire a bolt farther than anyone can shoot an arrow. Even ye." His eyes narrowed. "'Tis dangerous."

Kinsey's chest tightened. It must truly be dangerous if Drake, the most honorable man she knew, would share such information with his enemy. And he'd done it for her. To keep her safe.

She reached out and caught his hand. "Thank ye."

He looked at their joined hands for a moment, his expression hard. "I dinna like this."

She didn't know if he meant that he didn't like that he'd just told his enemy about their greatest weapon, or that his enemy was his own sister. Most likely, all of it.

Certainly, she hated the situation too. But not enough to go back to Castleton.

He had always been more forgiving of the English than she was.

His expression turned sad, and he ruffled her hair, the affectionate gesture half-hearted. "Stay safe."

"Ye as well."

He regarded her one last time, as though loath to leave. But at last, he slipped away, out of the alley and onto the main path running in front of the tavern where he disappeared.

Mayhap forever. Or at least from her life.

She'd known that by joining the effort to reclaim Scottish

land, she would be putting a strain between her and Drake. But she'd never thought the confrontation would happen so quickly. Or that it would harbor such permanence.

Something in her chest gave a painful twist.

"Kinsey." The masculine voice wasn't Drake, but still familiar.

Sir William.

Drake had thought she'd run off with him. How preposterous. As if Kinsey would ever sacrifice anything for a man, let alone her family.

Then she remembered how Sir William had threaded his long, tapered fingers through her own at the table. They'd been feigning lovers to avoid arousing suspicion. She hadn't expected Drake to see it as well.

The shadow of a man with a muscular physique appeared at the head of the alley. "Kinsey?" Sir William called.

She sighed and made her way to him.

"Did ye find something?" he asked, his brows furrowed quizzically.

"I needed some air." She strode toward, careful to avoid the greasy pools of stagnant water. "'Tis foul inside."

"'Tis foul here." He hesitated. "Did ye overhear something?"

"I beg yer pardon?" she asked innocently. Mayhap too innocently.

He tilted his head at her. Was he skeptical? Had he seen Drake?

Her pulse thudded in her ears.

"Ye have no' found anything then?" William asked.

She hesitated.

Kinsey was ashamed to admit there was a second, a splinter of a second, that she considered telling William what she'd heard about the weapon. But she knew what divulging that secret had cost Drake, what a blow it had been to his tightly bound morals.

She could never betray him.

"Nothing." The lie was bitter on her tongue. William and his men would be facing that weapon. It would put all of their lives in danger.

Regret balled like ice low in her belly. She wished she'd never seen Drake. It hurt her heart even to think that. She'd happily anticipated his visits in the past years. He'd always been so caring and supportive, knowing how to navigate her moods and never making her feel childish. And she wished to God he'd never told her about the weapon. Not when its knowledge burned like an ember in her mind.

Sir William glanced about the alley. "'Tis no' safe out here. Even for a lass who can handle herself." He extended his hand to her.

She looked at it, recalling how warm and strong his fingers had felt over hers. It hadn't been unpleasant to hold his hand. But she certainly wouldn't admit as much to him, nor would she take his offer now.

Instead, she simply strolled onward and pushed into the tavern at his side. The ladies within had a greater appreciation for Sir William than Kinsey. They immediately straightened when they saw him, their eyes raking down him with interest.

Kinsey shouldn't have bothered to notice but couldn't stop herself from glancing at the knight to observe his reaction.

He didn't bother to look at a single one.

Instead, he regarded her and gave that charming smile as he offered her his arm once more.

And this time, for some inexplicable reason, she accepted.

WILLIAM WAS PLEASED WITH HOW THE TRIP TO THE TAVERN had gone the night before. The knowledge they had gained on Mabrick Castle would be integral in planning their attack.

From the whole of what they had gathered, King Edward was well aware of King David's intent and sought to fortify his stolen lands. This meant that soldiers were being sent from England to Scotland. For example, those assigned to Mabrick Castle.

The forces were small, of course. The king was no fool. Especially when it came to a fortified border. However, many of those castles often had more guards than necessary. The number of men leaving for Scotland would still help William and his army take the castle. If nothing else, it meant a second round of rested Englishmen wouldn't be available to engage in battle once the first round grew tired.

After all, William had only fifty men and an archer. Which was why he had to be clever.

He gathered a group from his army, including Kinsey, to spy on Mabrick Castle. They arrived just before sunrise and hunkered down in the surrounding forest, the leaves on the floor still damp with morning dew.

He settled among the shadows with Reid at his right and Kinsey to his left. William was used to Reid and his steady, silent presence. The man was more stone than flesh, not making a sound even as he breathed and watched with sharp eyes, not flinching or moving.

William was far more aware of Kinsey. Not that she was loud, for she was quiet and still. Nay, it was the way her sweet scent lingered above the smells of wet earth, the whisper of heat from her body teasing along the left side of his.

She'd warmed to him at the tavern. Not initially, but when he'd followed her into the alley. Her smiles had been more genuine after, even touching her lovely eyes.

He glanced at her now and found her attention fixed on the castle wall with the focus of an archer. No doubt, she was assessing the crenellations for any sign of weakness, a place where she might be able to slip an arrow.

Which was exactly why William had wanted her with them.

For his part, he was keeping a mental tally of every soldier on the wall, noting how often they circled the perimeter and what weapons they appeared to be armed with.

As they watched the castle, Duff had been instructed to circle the large structure in an attempt to identify any other points of entry aside from the portcullis at the front. If there were none, William and his army would be forced to scale the castle walls.

He considered the fortifications in the event they were left with no other option. Somewhere in the foliage behind him, a twig snapped.

William's pulse jumped, but before he could even spin around, the creak of a bow being drawn taut came from his left.

Fib emerged from behind a cluster of trees, his hands lifted in surrender. "Dinna shoot. 'Tis just me."

He was speaking too loudly, standing upright and uncovered where anyone could see him.

"Get down," William hissed.

Fib ducked, awkwardly hunching his lanky frame as he swiftly made his way toward them in a strange bent-legged duck walk and collapsed on the forest floor between William and Kinsey.

"I dinna mean to startle ye," the lad whispered, wide-eyed.

"Ye could have been caught by the English." Anger welled up in William, spurred by fear. The lad had been trained for a battle, aye, but he wasn't yet adept at fighting. And he had received no instruction on spying or being stealthy.

William's chief concern was for the inexperienced lad. The boy had spirit and would never talk to the enemy. No matter how much they tortured him.

The very idea turned William's stomach. Once more, he experienced a surge of ire at his father and his insistence that the boy's offer to join William's ranks be accepted.

"Ye shouldna be here." William frowned at Fib.

The lad looked up at him with a bright, wounded expression. "But I'm always left at camp. I practice in every free moment I have, and even ye have said I'm a skilled swordsman. Have I no' proven myself?"

It was true. The lad had worked hard to sharpen his skills. And of anyone, William was more familiar with how painful it was for one's efforts to go unnoticed. It was when Fib's gaze slid to Kinsey that William realized the boy was further humiliated by being chastised in front of her.

"Am I wrong?" Fib demanded in an uncharacteristically stalwart manner, repeating, "Have I no' proven myself?"

William sighed. "Aye, lad, ye have."

Movement showed on the perimeter of the castle, calling attention to another guard going through his watch. Irritation for the situation tightened the muscles along the back of William's neck. He forgot how long it had been since he last noted a guard. Such information would be necessary for their attack, without room for a single error. They couldn't afford this distraction.

Reid stirred at William's side, his aggravation evident.

Fib did not seem to notice. "Let me join ye for the attack."

"Nay." William turned his attention to the castle once more. "Go back to camp."

"Fib," Kinsey said. "'Tis not safe."

His face went pink. "I'm no' a bairn. I'm a man, a trained warrior. Let me join ye as I'm supposed to."

Kinsey pressed her lips together, and William assumed even she was growing weary of Fib's begging. The worst of it was William had no true reason to leave him behind. Being too young was not a viable excuse. Most of the army was young, some only a few years older than Fib.

Still, it was on the tip of William's tongue to decline.

"Please." Fib clasped his hands in an earnest plea. "Please. I've worked verra hard for this. I want to join the men. And Kinsey." He shot her a grin.

"Fine," William said with resignation. But even as he spoke, an uncomfortable knot formed in his belly. The idea of the lad being in battle with the rest of William's army did not sit well with him. It never had, and it especially did not now.

Fib's beaming smile did not allay that trepidation.

William allowed the lad to stay with them while they scouted the castle, so long as he remained quiet. However, when Duff had finished looking over the perimeter and reported back that there were no additional doors outside of the main one, William had the older man return Fib back to camp.

This way, William knew the boy would be silent. Duff wouldn't tolerate anyone giving away their location and was gruff enough to not care about a lad's feelings.

William and the others stayed until afternoon, not leaving until their relief arrived to assume their positions. After relaying what they had observed, William, Reid and Kinsey headed back to camp on stiff legs. A spot low at William's back protested with a nagging ache.

"Ye shouldn't have told him he could fight," Kinsey said.

Reid merely cocked an eyebrow and kept walking.

Oblivious or uncaring, Kinsey stopped and crossed her arms over her chest. William stopped as well and faced her. "I assume ye're referring to Fib."

"I am." Her pale blue eyes glittered with determination, and sunlight danced off her red curls.

He wanted to thread his fingers through her tresses to see if they were as silky as they looked. No doubt, he'd get an arrow in his bollocks if he tried. "The lad has worked hard, as he said. I dinna have a reason to say nay aside from my concern at his age."

"Ye're in command. Ye could've said nay without reason."

"Do ye think he would have accepted it?" William met the challenge of her gaze.

She gave an irritated sigh and tossed her curls over her shoulder. It was answer enough. He knew she understood even if she refused to admit it. An idea struck him.

He resumed walking toward camp once more. "I'll have him stay back with ye."

"I beg yer pardon?" She rushed to catch up with him.

"He can stay back in the woods with ye. I've seen how he looks up to ye. Take advantage of that admiration and show him how to be a proper archer." William shrugged. "It will get him in battle like he wants but also keep him safe. Like we want."

She pressed her lips, quiet a moment as she considered. "Aye. I'll do it."

"Thank ye." He smiled at her in appreciation. Despite her fierceness, there was a tender side to her. It was a balance within her that appealed to him greatly. "Now, let's get some food."

Fib met them as they neared camp, his face bright with excitement. "We need to attack tonight."

His words took William aback. "What do ye mean?"

Duff joined them and scratched his thick dark beard. "We nearly ran headlong into several guards on our way back to camp. We were no' seen but overheard a plan to shift soldiers deeper into Scotland tonight. The replacements coming up from England are delayed by weather and willna arrive until the following day." He slid a look of irritation at Fib. "The lad is correct. If we want the advantage, we should attack tonight."

## 5

William gathered his men that night and made for Mabrick castle. Even as he did so, the action didn't sit well with him. He preferred more reconnaissance, a chance to understand better the activity and numbers within the castle.

However, not only did this night present fewer guards, the moon was blanketed behind a curtain of clouds, which would further mask their attack. It would be their best opportunity for victory. To squander such a chance would be foolish.

With only the main gate as an entry point into the castle, they would scale the walls with grappling hooks. Kinsey would be hiding in the outlying forest with Fib, shooting at the guards as they attacked William and his men.

It would not be an easy conquest. Taking a castle was always risky. William knew that. But if they could claim Mabrick Castle, William's worth would be proven to his king. And to his father.

They waited to attack until the dead of night when most would be sleeping. William and his men assumed their positions in the forest, crouched down in wait.

A lone guard walked the parapet, his head visible above the

crenellations. After he passed, time dragged on at an excruciating crawl as they waited for another. The whisper of leaves brushing against one another in the breeze was the only sound to be heard.

They saw no one else until the same man reappeared a while later. William waited until he had passed.

"Now," William said as loud as he dared.

His men were like hunting dogs straining at their leads, shooting off across the stretch of lawn to the castle. Their fiercest soldiers, including him, Reid and Duff, launched the grappling hooks simultaneously. They spun the weighted end three times and, with a nod to one another, sent the heavy iron sailing up into the sky and over the crenellations where they raked across the stone and held.

The sound was harsh in the quiet stillness, but it was swift, with each hook catching at almost the same time.

William tugged his rope to ensure it held. It did. He tightened his grip and put first one foot, then the other to the pockmarked stone. As quickly as he dared, he began to scale the castle wall along with several of his men.

He was nearly halfway up when the lone soldier gave a shout of alarm.

An arrow flew from the forest, and the cry was cut short.

There wouldn't be much time now. Hand over hand, William climbed, his gloves gripping the coarse rope with ease while his legs helped brace his weight.

"Cut the lines," one of the men called out.

The stomp of rushed footsteps came over the side of the wall, indicating more guards had arrived. Another arrow was launched from the forest.

"Faster," Reid ground out as he hastened.

William's arms and back were on fire with the effort of climbing; the soles of his leather boots gripped the wall to the best of their ability. Though they were close to the top, they still had some distance to go. His grunts of effort mixed with those of his men.

They were near enough now to hear which arrows missed as they skittered across the stone, and which hit with a quiet thunk and a gritted cry from its victim.


THE ROPE IN WILLIAM'S HANDS VIBRATED WITH THE EFFORT OF someone sawing at the thickly woven fibers.

His heart slammed harder in his chest, and he moved past the exhaustion of his muscles.

Finally, William reached the top. He threw one leg over the crenellation as he drew his sword, plunging it into the neck of a guard who was furiously cutting at the rope of his grappling hook. The man staggered back and fell.

A glance below confirmed Reid was two handgrips away from joining William, and only one other man, called Alec, held on to a rope near the top. William launched at the guard trying to slice through Duff's rope.

Reid was at William's side as he ran his blade through his opponent, followed by Alec and Duff, who arrived safely and without incident.

Five others joined them moments later, their swords flashing and slashing at the Mabrick guards.

All at once, there was an explosion from the right. The ground rumbled beneath William's feet, and the boom was so deafening, it left William with a high-pitched ringing in his ears. But it did nothing to dull his vision, nothing to shield him from the sight as a massive bolt punched through first one of his men, then a second. The thick stock of metal continued onward, glistening with their blood as it sailed into the night.

The two men had been standing near the edge and pitched over without once crying out—as they were dead before they fell.

A moment of shock descended on the battle, and for the blink of an eye, no one moved. Not William and his army, nor the Mabrick guards.

"Get the archers." The shouted order launched everyone back into action. Amid the ring of clashing weapons and roars of men was the unmistakable rasp of another bolt sliding into the weapon that had killed two men in one blow.

A cluster of eight guards rushed toward them, an amount they could certainly take.

The massive boom thundered once more, causing the stone beneath their feet to shudder. A heart-rending cry came from beside William, and he knew he'd lost another man.

*Damn.*

The attacking guards redoubled their efforts, forcing William and his men back. William braced himself but still found his heel hitting the hard stone wall behind him. He cut down the man in front of him, and his falling opponent was immediately replaced with a guard who was taller, stronger.

The man struck like an ox, each blow so hard it made William's bones rattle. Back, back, back, the man pushed as William's other heel met the stone.

An arrow flew past his shoulder and sank into the man's throat. Blood gushed from the wound, and the guard dropped. As he fell, William caught sight of an oblong iron barrel with a flame flickering at its rear.

*Boom!*

Fire flashed at its front as a massive bolt shot out. This time, however, it hit a crenellation with a splintering crack, taking a chunk out of the stone. Another English guard attacked William.

"They have an archer," one of the Englishmen called out.

The back of William's neck prickled in fear.

Beneath the sounds of battle came the familiar creak of a dozen bows being drawn. Only this time, William knew they would be pointed toward the woods, in the direction of Kinsey and Fib.

Kinsey kept her gaze locked on the top of the castle, where four of their men were nearly being pushed over the side. While she had never been in battle before, she knew this one was not going well.

She took aim and released her bowstring. Her arrow sped through the air and hit the guards trying to shove one of William's men to the ground.

Despite the grisly fate of their fellow fighters, the other men had not abandoned their attempts to scale the wall. Nine more were climbing to the top, nearly midway. Four men had been cleared away from the ground, victims of the *pot-de-fer*, and one due to an arrow. The rest of their army had backed into the safety of the woods and lay in wait for their turn at the ropes.

Fib fluttered around her in excitement and horror, his hands on his head. "There are more archers firing."

"I see them." Kenzie redirected her aim toward the bowmen shooting at the men edging up the wall. One of them cried out and fell, the silence of his descent indicative of his fate.

She released another arrow.

"Ye got one." Fib threw his arms into the air in victory.

All at once, she realized an archer had turned toward her.

Her pulse spiked.

They were shooting at her. At her and Fib.

"Down," she shouted as she dove toward the earth.

Fib joined her on the ground, partially covered by several thin tree trunks. The arrows whooshed toward them, cutting off abruptly in several errant thunks and pops as they landed harmlessly around them.

"Go to the forest where the others are," she ordered Fib.

He stood stubbornly in place. "Are ye coming?"

Another hearty boom cracked through the night, and yet

another man pitched over the side of the castle wall. Dead. More arrows rained down on the men climbing the ropes.

One cried out, and the group began to descend with haste as a call came to the archers once more.

Kinsey leapt up and took out another archer. While it was a victory, her shot let them know she was still alive. They would fire at her again.

Fib clambered to his feet with a cheer. "Ye hit one more."

"Go now, Fib," she said through clenched teeth. "The men are retreating. Hurry and join them."

"I willna go without ye."

One of the men loading the *pot-de-fer* lifted his head over the crenellations for a fraction of a second, and she released her nocked arrow. He ducked down, just as her carefully aimed arrow shattered against the stone behind him. Exactly where his head had been.

The men atop the castle fought onward with tireless strength. Doubtless, they didn't know their men were gone.

Several arrows sailed toward Kinsey once more. She ducked, pulling Fib with her. An arrow landed just before Kinsey's face, not even an inch from her eye. Her breath sucked in sharply. That had been close.

Too close.

All at once, the four men fighting leapt over the wall, catching the ropes and sliding down with haste.

Kinsey's stomach sank.

They were retreating.

They had lost.

The archers turned their arrows toward the ropes.

"Fib," she shouted in aggravation. "Ye need to leave now. We're retreating."

"Nay, my lady," he replied stoically. "A man of chivalry would never leave a woman alone to defend herself."

She loosed an arrow at an archer, who pitched crumpled out of sight. "I'm no ordinary woman."

But she couldn't think about Fib now, not when she had to concentrate on picking off as many archers as she could. She couldn't see to tell if one of those men was Sir William. Most likely, one was. After all, he rode at the head of the army and was always first for watch and reconnaissance. Aye, she did not doubt he was one of those now running for their life.

If Sir William died and his men disbanded, she would have no choice but to return home. Her intent to right the wrongs done to Scotland would have been a failure. The words of valor and bravery she'd written in her letter to her mother and sister would be lies.

She wasn't done fighting yet.

The men scrambled down the ropes amid a barrage of arrows. One stuck fast into one of the men. Thankfully, he didn't release the rope, his rapid descent not slowing.

"One of the men has been hit," Kinsey said. "Go to the forest to meet him. Help him get back to camp for aid."

Fib hesitated this time.

"He needs ye." She infused her statement with an urgency in the hopes of discouraging him from staying.

A strange sensation twisted in her stomach, and the hair on the back of her arms stood on end.

More arrows were flying toward them. She hadn't noticed early enough, as she had been focused on trying to get Fib to leave.

"Fib," she cried, her voice pitched with fear.

But rather than duck, the brave lad threw himself before Kinsey.

The arrows thudded into the forest. Fib jerked several times and issued a low, whimpering exhale as he sagged toward her. Bright red blossomed over the front of his gambeson, staining his chainmail where several arrows had gone through his slight frame.

Fib's stare slid down to his chest to the bloodstains that continued to grow.

"Nay," Kinsey screamed.

His legs collapsed, and she caught him before he could fall into the dirt. Hot blood washed over her hands and drenched her kirtle. So much blood. Too much. Several arrows jutted from his back, every one stuck fast inside his slender body, the heads intentionally small enough to pierce through the chinks of chain mail.

Fib whimpered against her ear, and her heart constricted.

"Ye'll be fine," she whispered.

It was a lie, but she repeated those words over and over, her mouth moving as her thoughts scrambled, looking for a solution.

He was too heavy for her to lift. And Clara had always been the one with knowledge of healing. Kinsey would have to drag him to the other men. Mayhap someone at camp could help.

She carefully released him to readjust her hold. The color had drained from his face, and his body was limp. Her breath rasped with panicked gulps of air.

"Ye'll be fine." She slung her quiver and bow over her shoulder, grabbed him underneath armpits as gently as she could—mindful of the arrows—and pulled. Kinsey used the power in her legs against his weight to pull him slowly through the forest.

His legs bumped over the ground, collecting leaves and pine needles, but he didn't make a sound as she continued to haul him.

Her heart slammed with urgency.

She had to get him to camp. The sooner he was there, the sooner someone could save him.

Her thighs shook with the effort, and her arms burned from hefting so much of his weight. But she didn't stop. She didn't slow. Not until she caught sight of the three men.

The familiar silhouette of William's wide-shouldered frame was the first one she noticed. "William," she cried out through her tears. "Help me."

The men startled at the sound of her voice but recovered immediately and rushed to her.

"Fib." William knelt by the boy, wincing as he favored one side.

"Let me," Reid said, joining William by Fib and turning the lad on his side so he wouldn't jar the arrows prickling out of him like macabre spines.

William glanced toward the other man. "Alec, run to camp and let them know we have an injury to be seen to." There was a grimness to his voice that made a knot tighten in Kinsey's gut.

Alec ran off through the forest at a frantic pace, leaving the four of them behind in the still night.

William lifted Fib's head, which had lulled as Kinsey dragged him.

"Ye have to help him." She couldn't keep the panic from her voice now. Her fear trembled up through her and made hot tears run down her cheeks. "He was hit with several arrows. All through the chest, he—"

"It went straight through." Reid looked up at her with, his face solemn.

Kinsey shook her head, trying to stop him before he said the words she dreaded most.

William rose and put a hand to her shoulder. "Kinsey." His voice caught. "Fib is dead."

## ❧ 6 ❧

The defeat was soul crushing.

It wasn't that William had let his father down in his failure to reclaim the land that once belonged to the MacLeods. That was the least of his concern.

It was the men he had lost. Six of his father's guards, good men who were tough fighters, cut down as they clung from ropes and shot with that damn weapon.

And Fib.

A knot of emotion lodged itself in William's throat and his eyes burned with tears he longed to shed for the boy. He swiped them away. Sorrow tangled with rage.

The lad's death had been senseless. Unnecessary.

Fib was too young to have joined as a warrior in the first place. William never should have allowed his father to harangue him into bringing the lad. It hadn't sat comfortably with William. He should have known better.

Even going into battle so soon had not felt right.

He ought to have listened to his gut.

His men had paid the heavy price with their lives. Men, and one lad.

William stared at the opposite side of the cave they'd taken refuge in.

The surrounding forest was thick and they were far enough away that if guards from Mabrick Castle tried to find them, it would be a challenging feat. William and his remaining army needed a chance to see to their wounds and bury their dead.

They were staying only until the afternoon before making their way to Edinburgh to meet with the king's troops, that castle having just recently been reclaimed.

William had been foolish enough to expect to join them as he celebrated his own victory.

Footsteps sounded at the mouth of the cave, but he didn't bother to look at who invaded his privacy. "Leave me."

"Not when ye have an arrow stuck in yer side."

The voice was feminine, familiar albeit slightly hoarse.

Kinsey.

He turned his face away from her to hide evidence of his grief. "I dinna even feel it."

Her sweet scent told him she was near. He didn't want her to see him like this. Defeated, with his heart buried under the weight of such terrible mourning.

"Has he been buried?" William ground out, dreading the answer. He hated the idea of Fib in the earth, his body cold and alone. It was too final.

Kinsey gave a slow intake of breath, loud in the quiet of the cave. "Aye."

Agony split open inside his chest. Never again would he experience Fib's eager smiles, his enthusiasm to be counted as a warrior, or the incessant chatter as he went on excitedly about his newly learned skills.

"Ye were right." William shook his head. "I never should have let him come. Not on the campaign and certainly not in battle."

Kinsey settled beside him. "He was a determined lad. Ye thought he would be safe. And it isn't yer fault." She paused, and when she spoke, her voice was thick. "I tried to get him to leave—"

"Nay." William looked at her fully now. "It wasna ye."

Her eyes were red-rimmed and swollen from crying. Understanding showed in her gaze. "Ye truly cared for him."

"He was a good lad." The anger welled up inside him once more. "And too damn young."

"He was," Kinsey agreed.

Their grief sat between them, emotion running like a current of energy beneath the companionable quiet.

After a time, she gently touched his arm. "Will ye let me look at that arrow wound now?"

He regarded her with renewed fascination. "I dinna know ye were a healer."

To his surprise, Kinsey gave a mirthless laugh. "I'm not. But apparently, no one else here is either, and I'm the only one who knows how to sew."

Wariness replaced his fascination. "Have ye sewn a wound before?"

"Nay, but how much different can flesh be than cloth?"

It was as good an answer as any. The wound at his side thrummed in time with his heartbeat, a reminder of its existence.

She was right. He needed her to attend it. He'd seen far too many men carried off by infection.

Their next recruit would need to be a healer.

With a resigned sigh, he lifted his shirt where the arrow had sunk into the left of his abdomen. Arrows were nasty things. Once they were in, they were the very devil to take out. If one pulled the shaft, the wax holding the head on would separate, leaving the barbed metal in the wound. This could only be removed with a scoop, a vicious thing that left the wound gaping.

The best way to go about it was to shove the arrow the rest of the way through.

She probed gingerly at his side, and the discomfort edged into his awareness.

"Reid fought well today." He watched her as he said it, not expecting a reaction. Especially since she hadn't mentioned William's friend again. Nor had either of them shown interest in the other.

She pulled a wicked-looking dagger from her back and expertly trimmed away the fletching of the arrow with a quick arc of her wrist. It was a clean cut, one that wouldn't splinter inside him.

"I suspect ye already know I'll have to push this straight through." Her eyes found his. God, but she was beautiful like this, fierce with determination.

"I thought ye said ye were no' a healer," he teased.

"I'm an archer." She smirked. "I know arrows. But my sister has knowledge of healing. I've learned a bit from her." Her brow raised. "A very little bit." She pulled the stopper off a wineskin.

The pop echoed around the cave, and the scent of whisky reached William. She offered it to him. "Drink first. Ye may want to make it a hearty swallow."

This was going to hurt.

God, how he hated arrow wounds.

With a resigned clench of his back teeth, he took her advice and drank generously from the wineskin. The alcohol burned down his gullet, and a pleasant heat threaded through his body. He handed the wineskin back. "Get on with it then."

"Another." She nodded to the whisky.

Broaching no argument at such instruction, he lifted the whisky to his mouth. No sooner had the liquid passed his lips than a powerful pressure came from the arrow shaft, followed by a brilliant pain as the head punched through his back.

He hissed a breath through his teeth and drank in earnest.

"Not all of it," she cautioned. "I'll need some for the wound."

"That will feel divine, I'm sure," he gritted out. "I'd rather drink it, ye evil lass."

She straightened and put her hands on her hips. "A thank ye would do nicely." She extended one hand toward him, and he gave her the wineskin. "Lay back on yer good side for me."

"All I have are good sides." He attempted a charming smile and stretched out on the cave floor.

She rolled her eyes. "Keep talking like that, and mayhap I'll actually enjoy this."

Whatever smart retort he might have come up with singed away as the alcohol poured over his injury like fire and made stars wink and fade in front of his eyes. A cloth wiped over his skin in delicate strokes.

His head spun, feeling too light to stay on his body.

Images of the men who had died rushed to the forefront in his mind. Along with gruesome memories. How the bolt had torn through the two men at once. How small Fib looked where he lay on the damp leaves of the forest floor, the wound in his chest glistening in the darkness. Kinsey's chainmail smeared with his blood.

He was gone. Dead.

And it was William's fault.

"Unless ye can dodge an arrow, 'tis not yer fault," Kinsey said.

William lifted his head to look at her, which sent the cave around him swaying. Had he spoken aloud?

"Fib," he replied earnestly. "The failure of attempting to capture the castle. We should have spent more time observing, and I knew better. 'Twas far too soon to go in. I sensed it but ignored my instinct." He leaned his head back and closed his eyes against a rush of nausea. "That damn weapon. If I'd have known..." His throat clenched around the swell of emotion. "Men died because of me. Fib died because of me."

Her ministrations paused for a brief moment. "Nay," she whispered. "'Twas not yer fault at all." She sniffled. "'Twas mine. I

55

knew about the *pot-de-fer* but didn't tell ye. I didn't realize how powerful it was. Or what it could do to a man."

William's mind whirled. "Ye knew?" He stared at her, incredulous. "Ye knew, and ye dinna tell me?"

She looked away. "I couldn't."

"Who told ye?" William's usual patience snapped at its weakest point. Aye, he could get more from her by being charming, but he couldn't help his anger when she could have spared so much death. "How did ye know?"

She silently shook her hand, clearly intent on not replying. That was when it came to him suddenly. The recollection of the man who had been staring intently at Kinsey at the tavern.

"The dark-haired man," he said. "At the tavern."

Her head snapped up, and he knew his guess to be correct.

KINSEY STARED AT WILLIAM INCREDULOUSLY. HE HAD SEEN Drake.

*When?*

She turned her attention to the wound once more. The arrow had passed through cleanly, and the whisky had appeared to dribble through the wound. Hopefully, it would help stave off any infection.

"Who is he?" William's breath was coming harder, evidenced by the tight clench of his stomach every time he exhaled.

Even in such a situation, it was difficult to ignore the flex of his body in the firelight.

She threaded a length of catgut through a needle and pretended she didn't notice his attractive physique. "It's difficult to explain. Now hold still."

Healing had always been Clara's job. Kinsey's only real assistance was limited to fetching water or bottles of herbs. Never had she needed to tend to someone herself. Her stomach roiled still after having to shove the arrow through William's side.

The tip of the needle hovered near the edge of his open wound and trembled with the slight shaking of her hand.

*It's like cloth.*

She drew in a slow, deep breath.

*Just like cloth.*

She pushed it to his skin, but it was not at all like cloth. It did not yield easily, requiring more pressure, so she was shoving with the might of her powerful archer's fingers. The needle popped through, and William's taut abdomen flinched in a display of lean bands of muscle.

The odor of whisky stung her nose, and the blood trickling from the wound flavored the air with the stink of copper. Her stomach churned anew.

The second stitch to the other side of the open wound was just as bad, as was pulling the catgut taut over the injury so that it closed. The next, however, was easier. Somewhat. And in a matter of time, heavy with careful concentration, she was finally done stitching the front entry and back exit of the wound.

Her jaw ached from gritting her back teeth, and her fingers ached from the effort to push the needle through. She withdrew a roll of linen from her bag, provided to her by Alec. Before she could unravel a strip of the binding, William sat forward, and his blazing brown eyes met hers. "It canna be all that difficult."

Her mouth fell open with incredulity. "Have ye ever tended to an arrow wound and stitched it up yerself?"

"I mean the man from the tavern."

And they were back to that. She'd meant to divert William from the topic, but it had been she who had become distracted.

"It canna be all that difficult to describe who he is." William's jaw clenched, and she knew he was enraged.

Could she blame him?

His men were dead because of her. So was Fib.

It was the latter that finally made her speak. "He's my brother."

"Yer brother." His expression was unreadable.

"He works for an English earl on the border." She looked down at the loosely rolled linen in her bloody hands. Guilt burned its way up from her heart. "I knew about the weapon," she whispered. "He told me. He wasn't supposed to tell me, but he did it because he wanted to protect me."

"Why dinna ye tell me?" A muscle worked in Sir William's sharp jaw.

"He's an honorable man, the most chivalrous I've ever known." She hated how paltry her excuse sounded. "This slight break in his morality was the only one I've ever seen in the entire lifetime that I've known him. And he did it for me. If word ever got out that he had told me, it would destroy his hard-won reputation."

"Then maybe he shouldna have told ye at all," William said.

"I wished he hadn't as soon as he did." The confession was bitter on Kinsey's tongue. "I didn't want to lie to ye. And I didn't want the men getting hurt."

Tension filled the silence between them, replacing impassioned words with the small pops and crackles of the fire. Kinsey slowly withdrew her hand from his and began to unravel the linen once more.

She'd expected anger, but it was not rage simmering in Sir William's dark gaze when they locked eyes once more. It was interest. "Would he do it again?"

"Nay," said with finality.

"Mayhap if ye went to him—"

"Nay." She refused to discuss the possibility. "Even if it means I'm dismissed from yer army."

William put a hand up in quiet surrender. "Ye willna be dismissed. Ye're too valuable as an archer."

His words eased some of the tension from her shoulders.

"I need to apply yer bandage." She held up the rolled linen. "Ye'll need to stand."

He did as she asked, his mouth tightening with pain slightly as he did so.

Kinsey put a thick fold of cloth over his injuries and wrapped a length of linen around his waist several times to ensure it would stay in place.

His gaze remained fixed on her as she worked. "I would have gone through with the attack anyway. Even if I'd known about the weapon."

Kinsey wound the linen around him, holding one end gently with her fingertips. "Would ye have?" Once done, she cut the bandage with her blade and secured one end of it by tucking it against the firmly coiled linen.

"Aye." He bent one leg up and rested his forearm on his knee. "'Twas a rare and tempting opportunity for the castle to have so few guards. The fault doesna lie with ye."

As kind as it was of him to say, Kinsey couldn't believe her decision to keep Drake's information had nothing to do with so much death. She gazed down at the remainder of the rolled linen in her palm.

William lifted her face, so she looked at him once more. "It wasna yer fault."

She searched his eyes, a rich, velvety brown, fringed with dark, thick lashes. He hadn't shaved in several days, and a fresh shadow of whiskers covered his sharp jaw. His lips were full, soft compared to the hard lines of his handsome face, and she found herself wondering what they would feel like against her own.

His hand moved over her cheek, caressing it with his rough fingertips. He looked like a nobleman with his costly clothes and ornate sword. But right now, in a dreary cave on the English side of the border, as both mourned the loss of their fellow warriors, each shouldering the blame, he was more attractive to her than ever before.

His thumb trailed down to her chin, and his lashes lowered as he watched his finger. Gentle as a whisper, he swept his touch over her lower lip, sending a small flutter through her pulse.

She liked his touch. She didn't want to admit it, but the tender brush of his skin to hers made her crave more. Her eyes closed as she gave way to the sensation. She wanted to tilt her face toward him but thought that might be too much of an invitation and resisted the urge.

"Beautiful Kinsey." His voice was intimate and low, sending goose bumps dancing over her skin.

Her lips were suddenly dry. She flicked her tongue between them, and he caressed her with his fingertip once more. It made her want to draw his finger into her mouth, to suckle the tip delicately.

He was overwhelming.

His undeniable attractiveness, the innate goodness in him that tried to assume the guilt, the pleasing stroke of his skin over hers, it was too much. And yet not enough.

Part of her wanted to lose herself in him, to replace the grief with something far more enjoyable.

As soon as she had the thought, it was replaced with the way the tavern wenches had swarmed around him. He was too charismatic to have discouraged them for long. She'd seen his type in the village far too many times before. Handsome. Charming. Sought after.

She would be another woman in a long line of those showing interest. Hadn't she brought enough shame to her house by leaving without warning? She would not also become a slattern.

Her eyes flew open, and she leaned away from his touch.

His brows flinched with confusion and then hurt before it was shoved behind a confident half-smile. "Reid?"

"I beg yer pardon?"

"Because ye are drawn to Reid."

Confusion addled her for a moment as she tried to figure out what he was referring to. Suddenly she remembered how she had initially discouraged his affection is by claiming to have an attraction to Reid.

"Aye," she replied. "Of course."

The little smile on his lips widened. "Ye lied to me about him, dinna ye?"

Heat touched her cheeks, and suddenly she felt like Clara again with her blushes. The thought of her sister immediately made her picture home and her Mum. A flash of regret pierced her heart.

Were they worried about her? Would they try to find her? What would Drake tell them?

No doubt, her mother would be heartbroken.

"Ye're right," she said at last. "I'm not interested in anyone. I'm a warrior, and I'm here to fight for Scotland." She pushed angrily up to her feet. "Not to become some man's leman."

Before he could protest, before she could be lured by the temptation to stay and indulge her curiosity, she left the cave and didn't bother to look back.

## ❧ 7 ❧

**W**illiam kept his distance from Kinsey as the camp disbanded, and they set off for Edinburgh. They would arrive early despite the four days journey to get there. It was time he'd initially planned on using to take Mabrick Castle.

He would not be attempting a second attack. Not with the guards now on high alert. And especially not when the first attack had come at so great a cost.

The tension around his chest was more than he could bear and made the dull ache of the arrow wound at his side pale in comparison. If he'd been forewarned about that damned weapon, he could have altered the way they broached the castle. They could have avoided so many deaths.

And Kinsey had known.

He glanced to where she rode on her own, her back straight and proud beneath a cloak against the onslaught of rain. She claimed not to be interested in him, but her reaction in the cave had suggested otherwise.

The way she'd closed her eyes when he'd touched her, how she'd licked her lips as though preparing for a kiss, the quickening of her breath when he grazed her bow-shaped mouth with his fingertips. Aye, he understood women well from years of thoroughly pleasuring them. He was aware when a woman was interested and when she was not.

Kinsey was most certainly interested.

William guided his horse next to hers. She stiffened.

Ah, then she was still upset.

"It was presumptuous of ye," he said.

She shifted her focus from the endless path cut through the forest ahead of them and slowly regarded him. The auburn curls framing her face were wet with the rain, dark and clinging to her fair skin. "What was?"

"Ye thinking I took ye into my army so I could have ye as my leman."

Her mouth parted in indignation. "I didn't..."

He raised a brow at her feeble protest. They both knew she'd said as much in the cave.

She narrowed her eyes at him, ever as feisty as she'd always been.

William angled his horse to pull a large branch hanging overhead in their path. A twinge at his side reminded him to have a care for his injury. "I took ye on because ye're a good archer. No' because I wanted ye."

He released the branch, and beads of water cascaded down from the leaves, joining the rain and spilling over him.

A flush colored her cheeks, all the more appealing by the knowledge she didn't often blush. Not like the other women with whom he'd flirted.

"I see." She swiped at the wet curls on her brow, pushing them back. A small white scar, the size of his thumbnail, was suddenly visible at her hairline. How had he not noticed that before?

"Ye're right," she said in the span of silence. "I was presumptuous. I assumed ye wanted to kiss me."

"Oh, I did." He was free with his admission, knowing none of the others on the trail around them could hear. Their words would be drowned out by the falling rain, and the thick cloaks pulled over everyone's heads.

Kinsey turned her wide blue eyes on him in surprise, and he chuckled. "Ye're a bonny lass. Of course, I wanted to kiss ye." He winked. "Mayhap more than that."

She pulled in a breath. Now her cheeks were nearly as red as her hair.

He grinned at the accomplishment. "But that doesna mean I want ye as my leman. Ye've far more value to me as an archer."

"I'm glad to hear it," she said primly. "I've no interest in being anything other than yer archer."

He hadn't imagined her response to him in the cave and thus was aware of the lie of her claim. But he didn't press the issue. Instead, he shifted the topic so their conversation could be left in her thoughts to simmer.

"Is yer mum English, or yer da?" He nonchalantly asked the question, as though it were merely a curiosity. And it was to an extent.

He needed to know where her loyalties truly lay. With an English clip to her words and a brother who worked for one of King Edward's earls, she might not be fully with Scotland.

William had been willing to brush aside the topic of her brother offering her information, but it was certainly not forgotten. Not when her loyalties could be questioned. And not when such knowledge could help a future attempt for Mabrick Castle end in victory.

Kinsey didn't answer right away.

"Ye know ye can trust me, aye?" He winked at her. Lasses always loved when he winked.

She frowned at him but still replied. "My da, but he's dead."

"I'm sorry to hear that," he said solemnly. And he was. Having grown up without a mother, he knew what it was like to lose a parent early in life. "I dinna know my mum. She succumbed to fever soon after my birth. Did ye know yer da?"

He popped open a wineskin of ale, took a sip, then offered it to her.

She accepted it with a nod of thanks. "I was young, but my brother was on the battlefield with him when it happened. My da was an English knight." She drank, leaning her head back, so her long, slender neck arched gracefully.

"Fighting the Scottish?" William surmised.

Kinsey lowered the wineskin and attached the dangling cork in the opening before handing it back to him. "Aye. We were living in England at the time."

Her lip curled slightly.

"I take it ye dinna enjoy living there?" he pressed.

She scowled and gazed ahead at the muddy trail. "I didn't like how they treated us after my da died. They wouldn't sell us food, and they refused work to my mum. We had nothing—she was a widow with four small children, and not one of them offered aid."

He couldn't imagine Kinsey as a helpless child. Nothing about her seemed helpless. But then, he knew well the cruelties of the English, even if he'd never gone hungry as she had. "Bastards," William muttered.

Kinsey's fingers tightened perceptively on her reins. "Aye."

The chirping songs of birds and the rhythmic thud of their horse's hooves on the forest floor filled the space between them.

The sky began to darken as the sun they couldn't see began to sink. They would be stopping to make camp soon. Which meant William needed to readjust the focus of their conversation.

"Why does yer brother work for an English earl?" He made the question sound like the idea had suddenly come to him, as though he hadn't been thinking of it since the cave.

Except that he had.

Kinsey scoffed. "He's got it in his head that he can be a knight like our da was." She shook her head in obvious aggravation. "They'll never accept him, but he'll never stop hoping."

"Ye dinna think we can get him to join us?" he asked.

She laughed at that. "Drake would never turn his back on the Earl of Werrick. Not for all the coin in the world."

"Has he no' ever considered being a knight for Scotland?"

Kinsey lifted a single shoulder in a shrug. "I don't think he's ever tried. He set his mind on an English knighthood and has never been drawn away since."

"Even if they're using him?" William rubbed at the back of his neck. "They'll do that. Use one's dreams against them in an effort to get anything they want."

He let his words sink in before continuing. "We're aiding the new king and restoring his kingdom. He will be verra grateful to those who come to his aid. I would no' be surprised if he granted knighthoods to many of his loyal supporters."

She didn't reply, but then she didn't need to. The seed had been sown.

If they came upon Drake again, William anticipated the conversation between brother and sister might go differently, and that Kinsey may persuade her brother to join them.

Having the detailed knowledge of someone who worked for the English would give William and his army a great advantage. And what could it hurt if it also helped a man finally achieve his dream?

☙❧

KINSEY HAD BEEN GRATEFUL FOR WILLIAM'S COMPANY. FIB'S loss had been felt in the oppressive silence of the journey and made her heart ache more than she could bear. What was more, she couldn't get the idea of Drake becoming a Scottish knight out of her head. Not after William rode ahead to plan out their stop with Duff nor when they made camp on the outskirts of a village just over the Scottish border. She saw to her horse and mulled over what Sir William had suggested.

If Drake helped them take back English land, he could finally have his dream. Her heart swelled at the thought.

She couldn't remember her father. She'd been too young when he had died. But she did remember how Drake had worked so hard to ensure they didn't starve. How he'd been younger than even Fib when he first joined the reivers. Kinsey knew what he did was brave but hadn't fully appreciated the danger.

Not until now.

He had sacrificed everything to ensure their safety and comfort. Even his morals in running with reivers. And now, when his work turned to the English, who had caused them so much pain over the years. All to ensure his family could live.

But what if he didn't have to?

What if he worked with Scotland instead?

She wished she could go back to that conversation they'd had at the tavern. That she could offer him the opportunity to join them, instead of returning to Werrick Castle.

Sir William approached as she finished feeding and watering her horse. "We're going to the tavern for ale and a hot meal. Do ye want to join us?"

Kinsey considered the offer. She didn't much care for taverns and all the drunk men inside.

As if sensing her hesitation, Sir William nodded toward Duff. "Otherwise, ye'll be left with whatever he cooks up on the fire." He grimaced.

Kinsey had to laugh at that. The night before had been a strange concoction of various plants Duff had found in the forest and cooked alongside roasted rabbit. The rabbit was good, tender meat and crisped skin. The forest plants, however, tasted exactly what one would expect forest plants to taste like. Dirt and disappointment.

She made a face. "Aye, I'll come."

William grinned, and her heart gave a funny little flip.

God help her if his charm was finally beginning to take effect.

They joined a group of William's men and walked the short distance to the tavern. It was as the other had been, dank and dingy, the air thick with tallow smoke and the pungent, undeniable odor of unwashed bodies. There were a few patrons within, but their party filled the place.

The serving wenches immediately made their way to Sir William, fluttering their lashes and plumping their bosoms. It hadn't bothered Kinsey before, but now she found every tittering giggle made the muscles along the back of her neck tighten.

William flashed his handsome smile but didn't flirt. Rather, his gaze kept creeping toward Kinsey, though, of course, she didn't let on that she noticed.

The ale at the tavern was different from what her mother made. Different even than what they'd had on the road. Stronger, with a sharp, nutty aftertaste. She didn't usually consume very much, but now found herself moving onto her third as her head began to spin.

The more she drank, the looser the band of tension around her chest became. Her thoughts had continued to swing back toward death for the better part of their journey. They had been put there by Fib's absence, by the decreased number of their army with the others they had lost.

And the men she had killed.

Mayhap it was cowardly of her, but she was glad the English guards had been at a distance. She didn't know if she could kill someone up close.

At the moment when she'd shot them, they had been targets, an opportunity to save one of her own.

But on the trail when she'd had too much time to think, she couldn't help but wonder at the children they might have had, the wives waiting for them to return when they wouldn't, the mothers whose sons were now dead. And Kinsey had been the one to rob them of their loved ones.

How many had she killed?

She combed through her recollection of the night and tried to count them, but it was impossible. Yet not knowing made it even worse.

"Kinsey?" William asked. "Are ye well?"

She straightened. "Aye, of course."

She was with men who had seen battle before, who had killed before. And among them, she was the only woman. She refused to say what was in her heart lest she be seen as weak.

Sir William's eyes lingered on her for just long enough to indicate he didn't believe her, but nor did he press the issue. Beside her, Alec had consumed more ales than Kinsey had bothered counting.

"Did ye see our archer in the attack?" Alec flung his arm over her shoulders. "No' only is she bonny, but her aim is perfect."

Kinsey's muscles were relaxed from the ale, and she didn't bother to push her fellow soldier off as he hugged her with brotherly affection, bringing with him the smell of stale sweat and ale. Sir William's eyes narrowed.

"I wager she could be the one to beat Sir William at throwing daggers finally," Alec boasted.

Kinsey lifted her brows at Sir William. "Are ye good with daggers, then?"

A smile lifted the corners of Reid's lips. "The best."

"I wouldn't say the best," Kinsey replied, thinking of her eldest sister. For all her gentle kindness, Clara had the accuracy of an assassin when it came to her daggers. If she could set aside her tender heart, she would be Scotland's most sought-after mercenary.

A low murmur of appreciation went around the table, and Kinsey realized belatedly they thought she had meant herself.

Sir William's eyes gleamed. "A challenge then?"

Kenzie opened her mouth to protest that she'd meant her sister, not her. She had some skill with throwing daggers, aye, but nothing like Clara. A cheer erupted from the men as they chanted her name.

Who could say nay to such a vote of support?

After all, her aim was true enough.

"I accept," she said with a boast of confidence.

Mugs of ale were lifted high, and men pounded on the table in approval. Alec's arm released her shoulders, and she rose from the table with Sir William.

"Shall we make this interesting?" He asked as he led her outside along with the others.

An old tree stump sat several paces from the tavern, its core scarred with pits and gashes from the many blades thrown at it over the years. They were evidently not the first to have such a competition.

"Interesting?" Kinsey looked up at him coyly. Maybe even with a hint of flirtation. Her head was light and her blood hot, both due to the ale she'd consumed.

And she liked it.

"A wager." He withdrew the dagger from his belt.

"Ah." Kinsey eyed his blade. It was a quality weapon with a straight, shiny blade and a smattering of what appeared to be rubies glittering at the end of the hilt. "If I win, I get yer dagger."

William glanced at his blade, contemplating. "Verra well. If I win—"

"A kiss," one of the men shouted. The following jeers supported the suggestion.

"I wouldna say nay to a kiss from such a bonny lass." Sir William winked at her. "Though I wouldna want ye to think I was only trying to make ye my leman," he said in a low tone, meant only for her.

A furious blush blazed at her cheeks.

It was a bold request. And one of little concern. After all, she *would* win.

She nodded. "A wager it is, then."

## ❧ 8 ❧

**W**illiam had competed in many throwing competitions in his life and had lost only once before, to a one-eyed man from Skye. It taught him never to underestimate his opponent.

He certainly didn't with Kinsey.

She was the kind of lass to look a challenge in the face and laugh. That confidence showed itself now in the upturn of her chin.

He indicated the stump and stepped back. "Best of three. Bonny lasses throw first."

Several men made lewd jests, which she responded to with a sharp look. The tavern kept a small bonfire burning for patrons who went outside for fresh air. It was by its flickering light that she aimed at the stump.

Kinsey pulled back her arm, paused for a brief moment and released the dagger. It sailed through the air and thunked into the center of the tree stump. A triumphant smile lit her face.

Someone whistled in appreciation.

William was next. He fingered the handle of his dagger, a gift from his father. One that he didn't plan on losing. It had been given years ago before his father had lost faith in him. Before William had stopped trying.

The dagger was a reminder that no matter what William did, he might never be good enough again for his da. And so, William had to be good enough for himself.

He tossed the dagger. The action was simple but still caused a flash of pain to flare up at his side where the arrow wound had been stitched. He would need to be mindful of that.

The blade he'd tossed sank into the wood directly beside Kinsey's blade.

They reclaimed their weapons.

"Nice throw," he said.

"Yers was no' so bad either." She winked at him, almost flirtatious. "And by the end of the night, that pretty dagger will be mine."

He shook his head. "I'll be kissing ye senseless."

She laughed. "Senseless?"

He merely lifted a brow and gestured for her to throw. She took a longer time aiming, but still managed to hit the stump. He used the opportunity to employ less force for his throw in an attempt to favor his wounded side.

The crowd watching them now wasn't merely William's men, but also several of the patrons from the tavern and a couple of serving wenches. The blonde one openly stared at him with interest.

After his last shot, she edged her way through the cluster of people toward him, standing far too close. Her forearm was warm and damp where it pressed against him and she smelled of ale. "Whether ye win or lose, I'll keep yer bedroll warm tonight," she said in a husky voice.

But it didn't matter how low she tried to speak; her brazen promise carried in the night air. Kinsey stepped forward and pulled back her arm to throw her dagger.

"Ye've no' ever had a woman who can give pleasure like me," the serving wench purred.

He doubted that but would have been more than eager to try her claim—if he'd never met Kinsey, that was. When she was around, all other women seemed to fade. They didn't have her fire, her glow.

She released her blade, which veered off, nicking the side of the stump before falling into the thick grass.

William extracted himself from the serving wench's insistent company. "I've another prize in mind." He gave her a smile to ease his rejection and joined Kinsey.

He lifted his dagger a little higher for her to see. "If I land this dagger in the stump, I win."

She folded her arms over her chest. "Best of five?"

In truth, he would play this game all night with her. He enjoyed their playful banter as they competed and the way her eyes glinted with their friendly rivalry.

Although he knew deep down, he couldn't best her. He hated the idea of crumpling her confidence, especially in front of the men. He was too skilled and never should have presented the challenge in the first place.

However, he must have hesitated too long as he decided how best to miss and make it appear accidental, for she lifted her brow. "Don't do it..."

He blinked down at her innocently.

Her eyes narrowed, far too perceptive for her own good. "If ye lose on purpose, I'll never forgive ye."

"My side." He cupped his hand over the wound.

She smirked.

He sighed in exaggerated resignation and leaned toward her, breathing in the sweet, delicate scent of her. "Then prepare yerself for a kiss, my darling Kinsey."

Though he'd said it in jest, the reality of it slammed into him. He would be able to press his mouth to hers, to sample her warm, sweet lips, to relish the feel of her body against him. His loins stirred. Suddenly it became much more difficult to focus on planting his blade in the tree stump.

He steadied himself, took aim and let go of his dagger. It missed the center with genuine error, but still landed in the stump.

The men around him cheered and whistled. The blonde tossed him a look that said it was his loss and disappeared back into the tavern. He didn't care. He'd lost nothing. In fact, he'd won.

He turned to Kinsey, who regarded first his dagger, and then him.

"It appears ye've won," she said.

He couldn't keep the smile from his face. "It appears I have."

She bit her lip and stepped closer to him. Her focus drifted downward to his mouth.

"Kiss," Alec shouted.

The other men took up the word in a chant.

Kinsey's breath quickened. As ever, she didn't back down. Instead, she lifted her chin while closing her eyes. Determined to face the kiss.

Resigned.

That was not the way one ought to be kissed.

She had to want it as bad as him. To *need* it.

"No' in front of all ye." William faced his men. "I canna have ye stealing my wooing tactics."

"Are ye worried about competition?" Someone shouted, and everyone laughed.

"Ales on me." William nodded in the direction of the tavern. "Off with the lot of ye. But dinna stay out too late. We'll be leaving in the morn."

"Aye, Mum," someone else called, and more laughter rose.

William rolled his eyes playfully and shepherded them all inside.

He returned to Kinsey, who appeared as sheepish as he'd ever seen her. Or rather never thought to see her.

She bit her lip again, her fingers twisting against themselves. "Ye didn't have to do that."

"I'll no' kiss ye in front of those louts." He offered her his arm. "No' when it made ye anxious."

"I'm not anxious." She accepted his arm and slid her hand into the crook of his elbow.

He knew her to be a resilient lass, but her hand was delicate where it lay against his large arm. The heat from her palm whispered through his sleeve and to his skin beneath. Suddenly he wanted to kiss her then and there, to nudge her back against the tavern wall and let his hands and mouth roam over her until she cried out in breathless whimpers in his ear.

His cock swelled in his trews.

He guided her back to camp. "Kissing isna for public exhibition."

"Oh?" She was teasing him now, having recovered her poise.

It made him grin. "Aye, kissing should be private. A quiet, suspended moment in time between a man and a woman, hearts racing, breath coming too fast, bodies hot and alive with passion."

"Like that?" Her whisper coaxed his arousal.

"Aye," he agreed. "Like that."

They were near the camp, close enough to smell the earthy scent of whatever Duff had concocted from the forest for supper. A reminder they'd been better off at the tavern.

"We need to be somewhere we can be alone." He searched the still woods around them, cast in the subtle silver glow of the moon, and stopped. "Somewhere like here."

"Here?" She turned to him, her eyes wide and innocent.

"Have ye ever been kissed before, Kinsey?"

"Of course, I have." She answered so readily that he knew she was lying.

"Did ye like it?" He ran his fingertips down the delicate smoothness of her cheek, tracing the line of her jaw.

Her lips parted slightly, but she didn't reply.

"Ye'll like my kiss," he said in a low tone. "If ye want it."

"After ye rightly won?"

"I'll no' take what isna freely given." He trailed his finger under her chin, gently tilting her face upward. Moonlight washed over her fair skin, making her luminous. "Do ye want me to kiss ye?"

She swallowed.

"I willna expect ye to become my leman over just one kiss." He skimmed his touch over her bottom lip.

She exhaled a small laugh. "I'd imagine not."

He stepped toward her, near enough that his right foot went between hers and slipped his hand farther to cup the nape of her neck. "Do ye want me to kiss ye?"

Her eyes flashed with that boldness he liked so much. "I want ye to stop asking me and just do it."

That was all the answer he needed, and he lowered his head to hers.

&#9758;&#9758;&#9758;

KINSEY'S HEART POUNDED WITH A FORCE THAT THREATENED TO punch it through her chest. Sir William's palm was warm where he cradled the back of her neck in his large hand. There was a spiciness to his scent, something utterly masculine.

She lifted her face to his and closed her eyes, unsure what to expect.

She'd lied about having been kissed. She'd never bothered to waste time on dalliances. Not when there were so many other things so much more important.

His lips closed over hers, tasting the sweet ale they'd consumed. His mouth moved, as if he were sampling first her top lip, then her lower. Pleasure tingled over her skin, thrilling and visceral. She made a small sound in the back of her throat. A whimper? Or a moan, mayhap?

She couldn't think straight as he continued to brush their lips against one another. Her pulse thundered in her ears and throbbed an unfamiliar heat between her thighs. It embarrassed her to have such a powerfully intimate reaction to this man. But it also filled her with a longing to find out if it could go deeper.

And how much more so.

His tongue teased over her lower lip. She parted her mouth in surprise, and his tongue brushed against hers. This time the sound in the back of her throat was not so small.

He gave a low growl, and his other hand found her waist, drawing her against him as his kiss deepened further still. It was a primal, hungry need that echoed her own lust.

*Senseless.*

Nay, this wasn't an absence of senses; it was an explosion of them. Overwhelming in the most decadent way.

Emboldened, she met the stroke of his tongue and arched toward his solid body. Her hand rested on his firm chest, where his heart within pattered with frenzy. Like hers.

She wanted to feel him everywhere, to feed this new, exquisite desire.

He groaned. It was a low, desperate sound that reverberated in his chest and made her skin tingle with goosebumps. His mouth trailed down her jaw to her throat, raining kisses in his wake. Delicate ones, suckling ones, titillating flicks of his tongue over her skin that made her ravenous for more.

She clung to him, moving her body against his in a rhythm she couldn't control. His hand smoothed up her side to her breast, which he cupped in his palm. His thumb swept over her nipple, where it strained with sensitive eagerness, and her knees nearly buckled.

He held her more tightly, keeping her upright with his

powerful strength. Their bodies were so close that the hardness in his trews was evident where it pressed into her belly.

She had enough knowledge of men to know what that meant. But his arousal didn't repel her. Nay, it made a thrill of pleasure dance through her, that she could drive so handsome a man to such a state.

Her body had become highly alert, making her keenly aware of each touch, kiss, lick. His mouth was on hers again, their breath panting with the same lust, their teeth and lips grinding as their tongues sought to plunge deeper.

He stopped abruptly and rested his forehead to hers.

Kinsey's heart continued to race, her blood hot with the wondrous sample of lust. She wanted to ask why he'd stopped, to beg him to touch her again, kiss her again.

But she'd already made a fool of herself once by assuming he'd brought her on as his leman. It wouldn't do to play the part of the wanton now.

"*Jesu*, Kinsey," he whispered in a gravelly voice. "I dinna mean to do more than simply kiss ye."

Her cheeks burned, and her mind spun with the dizzying mix of alcohol and hot, raw lust.

He straightened and gave her a long, lingering look, his eyes bright in the splash of moonlight filtering in through the trees. His chest rose and fell with his frantic breathing.

He wanted her.

Not like the drunkards at the market. He'd had even fewer ales than she. Nay, he wanted her in the simple, sensual way a man yearned for a woman. And she longed for him just as ardently.

He smiled then, the charmer smoothing over his ruffled control. "If ye ever want to challenge me to daggers again, I accept."

"I'll keep that in mind." She tried to infuse her reply with as much nonchalance as she could muster.

"Shall we return to camp?" he offered her his arm.

It seemed ridiculous to be so formal when they'd just been so familiar.

Especially when it wasn't his arm that she wanted.

She accepted, nonetheless. This time, however, she noticed the power of his muscled forearm beneath her hand. It was all she could do not to stroke her fingers over his sleeve, to caress his body in any way she could.

The fire that had been set ablaze within her made her crave so much more. Kisses, touches, something—anything—to allay the need throbbing between her legs.

She wanted him so badly, in fact, that she realized she must do everything to discourage him, lest she fall into his bed and headlong into his heart. Such things would be far too dangerous.

"I only kissed ye because of the wager," she said. "This changes nothing."

"Dinna worry." He winked at her. "I dinna assume otherwise."

She experienced a flash of disappointment at his reassurance but nodded. "Good."

They arrived back at camp several moments later. A pot hung over the campfire, a grassy scent in the air. Sir William strode to it and ladled a bit out, revealing dripping strands of green-black plants.

"Duff?" He looked up at the stocky man.

"Dandelion leaves and nettles with a bit of squirrel." Duff puffed his barrel chest out. "Dinna look at me like that. 'Tis good for one's humors."

"I'll take yer word for it." Sir William let the ladle fall back into the pot.

Duff waved him off.

Kinsey settled by the fire, and Duff regarded her with a raised brow. "Only the two of ye?"

There was an implication in his suspicion. A justified implication.

Her cheeks went hot, and she was grateful he couldn't witness the extent of her embarrassment. "Aye, the others stayed behind," she replied with what she hoped was breezy indifference.

For his part, Sir William played as though nothing had happened, laughing and joking with the men who had remained back at camp. As if he hadn't made something inside her melt, as if the heat of awakened lust weren't still humming in his veins as it did in Kinsey's.

She forced herself to join in until she could finally retire for the night.

As soon as she closed her eyes, however, she was inundated with the memory of William's mouth on hers, the way he'd touched her breast, how his tongue had teased against hers. Hot frustration throbbed at her core. It was a curious sensation that was pleasant and achy all at once.

Regardless, she would do well to stay clear of William, for he was far too tempting.

## 9

William could not get Kinsey out of his mind. Not the night after the dagger throwing contest, nor any day or night thereafter as they traveled to Edinburgh.

It was far too difficult to douse that blaze of passion that seared his thoughts. She'd never been kissed before him. He'd been able to tell by the initial clumsy flicks of her tongue against his.

She was a fast learner, though, her body acting with an instinct that set his blood alight. A woman of incredible passion.

His cock stirred, as it did far too often now. It woke him in the middle of the night, painfully hard with desire. It was there in the morning, too, greeting him to a new day of unsatisfied lust.

*Damn desire.*

The journey took longer than anticipated due to an abundance of rain that left the roads thick with sucking mud. By some miracle, William's wound didn't get infected despite the dismal conditions. Indeed, it had begun to heal nicely with a pink, new skin slowly closing over the injury.

It was a good thing they did not try their luck at Mabrick Castle again, else they would have arrived late. As it was, the hulking form of Edinburgh Castle appeared on the horizon the day they were due to arrive.

The castle had been reclaimed some months before by King David's cousin, Edward, which made it the perfect meeting place for their impending attack on Lothian.

William's father would be waiting for him in those thick castle walls. The thought was enough to wilt even the hardest of cockstands.

Reid rode up alongside him. "I see yer kiss dinna win her over."

William glanced to where Kinsey rode, straight-backed and determined as any warrior, her gaze focused ahead. She hadn't so much as turned in his direction all day.

Mayhap he'd gone too far by kissing her silky throat or taking her fine breast in his hand. She'd been firm and full in his palm, her nipple taut, as if eager for the heat of his mouth. And she had moaned with pleasure when he'd caressed her.

She hadn't pulled away. He wouldn't have persisted if she had.

Indeed, she had ground her body against him, stoking the inferno of his desire with each flex of her pelvis against his.

William lifted his shoulders in a shrug, as though he didn't care. "I'll have to try harder next time."

Reid smirked. "If ye think there will be one."

William let his gaze linger on her as he recalled for the countless time the eagerness of her kisses. "Ach, aye, there will be."

He said it with such confidence, he almost believed it himself.

After all, he'd always attracted women. It was effortless on his part. They'd seemed drawn to him. Until Kinsey, who appeared absolutely unaffected by him. The more he tried, the less she cared.

At least until that kiss.

The longing nearly drove him mad. He wanted to kiss her again, hold her again, take things further than he had the first time.

All too soon, they were riding through the slanted streets of Edinburgh, making their way up the steep hill toward the castle. Toward William's father.

William allowed his army free reign of the city, with instructions to meet back at The Pig and Pony, an inn he'd stayed at previously. The place had good ale and was mostly free of vermin.

Among those who dispersed was Kinsey, without even a backward glance at him.

Reid stayed at William's side, as he always did. They arrived at the castle and deposited their steeds with a stable lad. Inside, the halls bustled with activity, suggesting the king had already arrived as well.

"William." The familiar voice coiled around William's chest and squeezed.

He turned to find his father making his way toward them in an immaculate red tunic embellished with gold thread. His thick gray hair fell to his shoulders in purposeful waves.

Laird MacLeod was a proud man. Proud and cold.

They met without embracing. "I trust ye have a victory to announce," his father said.

William's heart sank, knowing the disappointment he would lay at his father's feet. Dread washed over him like an icy wave.

He shouldn't care, damn it. He wasn't a lad anymore. He was a man, one who made careful decisions, who put his men before glory.

"I see." His father's gray eyes narrowed. "I'd like to speak with ye." He redirected his glare at Reid. "Alone."

Reid inclined his head. "Aye, Laird." He cast a quick look at William, as though wanting to lend his support and decline the laird's offer. In the end, he said nothing and turned toward the Great Hall.

Laird MacLeod led William up the winding stairs to a small private room. Though nearly the size of a privy chamber, the quarters that William's father was given to stay within was an honor. William, however, would be sleeping at the Pig and Pony, along with the rest of his men.

Once the door was closed, William's father turned toward him with such vigor, his tunic rippled. "There was no victory, I take it?"

"No' on our first attempt."

"There was a second?"

William squared his shoulders. "No' yet. The guards were alerted to our presence, so I thought it best to come to Edinburgh rather than engage in a second attack. Lucky that we did, else we'd no' have made it on time."

His father lifted his chin. "Ye failed."

William could have offered excuses. Especially in regard to the new weapon the English had used. "'Tis only failure if I stop trying. I intend to go back. And next time, I will be successful."

Laird MacLeod shook his head. "Ye take after yer mum. Her head was in the clouds more than on the ground, like ye." He frowned with disapproval. "Men canna have the luxury of such distracted focus."

"Dinna speak of her in such a manner," William said, raising his voice.

His father smirked. "Ye dinna even know her."

"I know she gave her life for mine." William glared at his father. "And I know she had fortitude enough to endure yer cruelty."

Laird MacLeod's mouth opened in outrage.

William put up a hand to stop anything his da meant to say. "I'm too damn old to care for yer approval."

His father smiled knowingly. "Ye're never too old to stop caring for my approval."

Rather than argue further, William turned and left the small room, refusing to give his father the satisfaction of seeing that he was right. Reid waited for him downstairs and lifted his brows in silent question when William approached him.

"It went as expected," William replied.

"Ale?" Reid asked.

"Aye."

Ordinarily, William would also want a woman or two with his ale, lusty lasses to drain the tension from his body with a long night of debauchery. But now there was only one woman he wanted.

The one he clearly could not have.

KINSEY HAD BEEN TO EDINBURGH ONCE BEFORE. A LIFETIME ago. It had been when she and her family traveled to Scotland from England after her da's death. She remembered the city being large and overwhelming.

But it hadn't just been the eyes of a child who saw it that way, for it was the same now. Buildings were pressed together and rose high in the sky as people rushed this way and that, their pace hurried. An unmistakable fetid odor hung in the air, so great it could only be produced by an area so populated.

She explored the city on her own for a bit with her dagger tucked close in her belt and her bow and quiver slung over her shoulder. But no matter what shops she discovered or the sweet currant and honey pastry she'd eaten, she couldn't stop thinking how much more enjoyable it would be to do with someone else. Her mum or Clara.

Or even Sir William.

Her stomach fluttered. He'd tried to flirt with her after the night of their dagger throwing competition. His wink had left her pulse racing, and the grin on his lips made her want to press her mouth to his. But she'd maintained a cool air. She had, after all, been the one to lay down the declaration that nothing would change between them after that kiss.

But it had.

Oh, it had.

At night, it inundated her dreams with heat and temptation. During the day, it chased away most other thoughts. And through it all, her body raged with desire.

After her time exploring, a sunset streaked the sky with fiery red, orange and purple over the city. It was then the day's drizzle became a hearty rain and forced her back to the Pig and Pony Inn for a hot meal and a dry kirtle.

By the time she'd changed and squeezed as much moisture from her curls as possible, she made her way downstairs, where the tantalizing scent of savory stew emanated. The tavern wenches were clustered around one table in particular, and she caught the familiar face at their center.

Sir William.

He drew women like shite drew flies.

Kinsey had thought herself different, immune to his charms. But now she was well aware that she too was just another lass under his spell.

Irritation tightened through her. She strode past him and Reid with a nod to them both and took a seat along an empty bench by herself.

Her bum had not even warmed the wood beneath her before Sir William appeared beside her table. "Mind if I join ye?"

"Ye already have."

He grinned. "So I have."

"I'm sure ye're disappointing many lasses by being with me," she replied dryly.

"What lasses?"

One of the very women she'd referenced approached their table and set down two mugs of ale and bowls of stew, as well as a platter of crusty bread. The ones delivered to Sir William were decidedly more carefully placed than Kinsey's.

"The lasses who notice ye everywhere ye go," Kinsey replied.

"There's only one woman I noticed tonight." He gave her his full attention, and her heart stumbled over its quickened beat.

She took a sip of ale to hide his effect on her.

The drink was cool with a nutty taste and a sharp bite at the end. Exactly what she needed. She lifted her brows at him in question.

"I've noticed ye." He ignored his stew and drank a hearty swallow of ale.

It was then she realized he'd most likely had several already before she arrived.

"Aye," Kinsey said skeptically. "Tonight."

"And the night before as well, and the one before that." He tilted his head, and a lock of his dark hair fell over his brow. It was unfair how even something so small was so becoming and enhanced his attractiveness. "I've noticed only ye since I met ye, Kinsey."

His words left a pleasant heat unfurling in her stomach. Damn him.

"How many ales have ye had?" She eyed his mug pointedly.

"No' nearly enough to make ye leave my thoughts."

He gave her a lopsided smile, and her heart quivered.

"Ye've a pretty tongue on ye," she scoffed.

He leaned closer and met her eyes with a burning heat. "I've a wicked tongue."

Her breath caught. The way he'd kissed her rose in her mind, his tongue stroking hers, teasing over her skin.

She took a bite of the stew to keep from having to reply. The meat was riddled with fat and tough as shoe leather, but the gravy was flavorful and the meal warm.

A serving wench approached them, her eyes wide and doe-like as she regarded William. "Anything I can get for ye?"

And by "ye," she obviously meant him. It was all well and good, for Kinsey would be retiring to her room after she finished eating. Away from Sir William, who was becoming harder and harder to resist.

He shook his head without glancing at the woman, and she shot Kinsey a petulant look before huffing away.

"Be honest with me, Kinsey." William eyed her earnestly.

Something told her she wouldn't like his query. She took another bite of stew, eager to be done and back in her room.

"Did ye enjoy my kiss?" he asked.

She drank from her ale to keep him from seeing the heat scorching her cheeks. When she set the mug down, she offered a shrug. "It was a kiss."

"But did ye—"

"I'm yer archer," she said, reminding him as much as herself. "Nothing more."

She scraped up the last of her stew with a bit of bread. "I'm tired." She rose from her seat, and he did likewise.

"Allow me to walk ye to yer room." He gave a little bow.

She scanned the room to see if anyone noticed. No one appeared to be looking at them, save a redhaired serving wench who was scowling in their direction.

"That isn't necessary." She headed for the stairs, and he quickly joined her.

He met her accusatory look with one of innocence. "I'm tired as well."

He was near enough that she could smell the wonderful masculine spice of him. Truth be told, she liked him at her side, and so she offered no further protest as he followed her to her room, where he paused outside the door.

She opened her mouth to bid him goodnight when he reached up to her face and gently caressed her cheek. She stilled, knowing she ought to pull away.

And yet, she found she was unable to do so.

"Ye're so verra beautiful, Kinsey," he whispered. "I canna stop thinking about ye."

Her breath came faster. Would he try to kiss her again?

Would she let him?

She could imagine him too perfectly, lowering his head to hers, the heat of his mouth brushing over her lips. Her pulse quickened.

"Did ye like my kiss?" he asked quietly.

How could she deny it when he was so near? When she craved him so desperately?

"It isna a matter of liking yer kiss or not," she said. "It's a matter of who ye are and who I am."

"So ye did like it?"

Kinsey sighed in irritation at herself for being honest with him. "Aye."

"We could do it again." He gave an arrogant smile.

She ought to have hated his reaction, but it only endeared her to him more. "Kiss?"

He hummed in reply. "And more." He leaned toward her and rested his arm against the door above her head, his solid body lightly pressed against hers. "I saw yer blush when I mentioned my wicked tongue. Did ye wonder what I might do with it? How I might give ye pleasure?"

The familiar heat of lust whipped up through her like a firestorm.

"Did ye wonder what part of ye I might taste?" His breath tickled her ear and sent prickles racing over her skin.

*Oh, aye.*

"Nay," she heard herself say.

He backed up to look at her. His high cheekbones left shadows on the chiseled structure of his face, and his eyes were dark with lust. It would be so easy to kiss him, to shed her excuses and draw him into her room.

But Kinsey had never respected those women who easily fell prey to a man's charms. While she had never truly understood the draw of lust before now, she still refused to act on her passions.

She had a task to perform, and if she were to be respected as a warrior, she could not also be a lover.

"Ye must stop," she said.

He straightened from her, immediately putting space between them. "If ye want me to stop, I will."

Her reply caught in her throat while her head and her heart warred for what response might emerge.

He waited patiently at a respectable distance for her answer. In the end, all she could do was nod.

Because she didn't want him to stop. But she knew she must be firm in her decision.

It was the idea of someone seeing him leave her room, of the men knowing of their lust for one another, which influenced her decision most. For them to look at her as though she was little more than a woman to warm William's bed, when she'd worked so hard to become a warrior. One who had earned the men's respect.

His gaze lingered on her a moment too long, and then he bowed politely. "Sleep well, bonny Kinsey. I will see ye at practice in the morn." He straightened and walked away, leaving her alone in the hallway, burning with shame and lust.

## 🕸 10 🕸

**W**illiam tossed and turned through the night. He'd anticipated sleeping in a real bed earlier that day. No matter that the mattress was lumpy and the straw inside in dire need of replacement. At least it wasn't the ground.

And then he'd gone and blundered things with Kinsey. He'd been arrogant in his assumption that he could kiss her again, that they might enjoy a night in a bed together. He'd like to blame his poor decision on ale, but he hadn't had all that much.

Not enough to lose himself.

Nay, that part had come from his attraction to her. Her curls had been damp when she'd come downstairs, the fiery locks darkened with moisture. She'd given him and Reid a quick nod of acknowledgment and bypassed William. God, but she drove him mad with her indifference.

It was those thoughts and many more that burned through the night and kept slumber at bay.

By the time he'd finally fallen into a restless sleep, the sun was already slanting through the shutters. When he managed to rouse himself, he realized with a sinking stomach that he was late to meet for practice.

He quickly dressed for the day and ran from the inn. The air was thick with the promise of more rain. He was able to arrive at the field outside the castle walls before the rain began to fall. Laird MacLeod was already there in front of the army, issuing commands with smooth authority. Though he wasn't loud, his voice carried, and his instructions were obeyed.

But then, William's soldiers were well trained.

His father faced him, and William's stomach dropped.

"Were ye able to secure the rooms for several additional nights?" he demanded.

Behind him, Reid winked.

William sent his friend a silent word of thanks and nodded with confidence. "Aye."

"These foul cities." Laird MacLeod's lip curled. "Always so damn busy. Again," he called out to the soldiers.

They swiped their blades in a simultaneous arc. Including Kinsey.

Where had she even obtained a sword?

"They're all in good order." Laird MacLeod gestured in her direction. "Except that one. What possessed ye to bring yer whore on as a soldier?"

It was said with disdain, the slur indicative that she wasn't worthy of traveling with them. Heat scorched up from his gut. At that moment, hearing that word practically spit from his father's mouth, William understood Kinsey's determination to refrain from an affair.

"She's no' a whore. Ye put an archer in a soldier's place." William folded his arms over his chest. "She's the best I've ever seen."

His father's brow quirked with interest. "Is she?" He returned his attention to her once more with renewed focus.

"Kinsey," William called out. "Get yer bow."

She moved with swiftness to comply with his request. The target was set up on the opposite side of the field. She looked at William, and he nodded.

Quick as lightning, she sent five arrows down the field, sinking each one into the target. Her fingers were deft as they plucked the arrows from her quiver, nocking each one with certainty.

Laird MacLeod nodded in approval. "Talented and bonny." He narrowed his cold eyes at William. "And ye're no' bedding her?"

"Nay," William replied, grateful that he was honest in his reply.

He studied her a moment. The rain had made her curls wild and lovely, and the chill in the air left her cheeks and tip of her nose red. Aye, bonny indeed.

His da smirked and strode off in her direction.

William was no fool. He knew exactly what his father intended to say to her. And even if William could have stopped him, he wouldn't have. Not when this would be so entertaining.

Laird MacLeod approached Kinsey. His hand lightly touched her lower back. She spun around, eyes flashing.

William didn't bother to hide his grin.

She propped one hand on her hip, her head tilted to the side with obvious impatience. Whatever his father said must have come to an end—or she interrupted him—as she leaned forward and spoke angrily to him.

Laird MacLeod turned away from her sharply and resumed to his place beside William, his face nearly purple with rage. "'Tis no wonder ye've no' taken her into yer bed. The lass is a harpy. Get rid of her."

William scoffed. "She's intelligent, and she's skilled. I'll no' get rid of her because she has the good sense to keep out of yer bed. Mayhap ye ought to have treated her like a warrior rather than a doxy."

"'Tis what she said." His father glared daggers at him. "I liked ye better when ye were bedding lasses rather than hiring them as warriors."

"Ye never liked me at all, Da." William cast a rueful look at his father before moving to correct Alec on a defensive move.

When he returned, his father was gone. No doubt to sulk in the shadows of the castle.

For the next several days leading up to the raid on Lothian, William kept his distance from Kinsey. She, of course, did not approach him either.

But he didn't stop thinking of her, dreaming of her, replaying in his mind the way she'd grudgingly admitted that she'd enjoyed his kisses. That wasn't all. He reminded himself how his father had said, "whore."

Their brief stay in Edinburgh flew by quickly as William worked with several other men commanding armies, all alongside the young king, in an effort to plan the raid. They would attack at all angles with fire and blades and arrows. The Englishmen inhabiting Lothian would fall.

The next morning brought the day of their raid on Lothian. William's army was armored and ready for the attack. Energy hummed in his veins, the way it always did before a fight, his senses heightened and on high alert. Aware of his restlessness, his horse shifted its weight from one hoof to the other, eager to charge at full speed.

They rode the short distance to Lothian in a tight group, surrounded by many other armies fighting for Scotland. Several had left early that morning and were already fighting. William's was one of the last groups to join.

His heart thundered like a war drum in his ears. His stomach clenched.

He hated raids and avoided them at all costs. Even now, in a moment where it was forced on him and his army, he would only fight English guards. Men who were armed. He'd instructed every one of his soldiers to do the same.

Kinsey, however, had been told to stay just outside of town. Archers had no business in close combat. Especially not with a raid.

The men ahead of William's army swept into the city like a swarm of locusts, their path set on destruction.

Lothian would surely fall.

⚜

KINSEY WOULD FINALLY MAKE THE ENGLISH PAY. CRACKLING energy raced through her like lightning until she was practically shaking. She gripped her reins tighter as if doing so could squeeze the excess tremors of anticipation.

The helm was heavy on her head and made her breath echo against the metal around her. From the slit in her visor, she could make out the city ahead of them, a cluster of tightly packed buildings, white-washed with thatch roofs. Plumes of dark smoke rose in various locations as homes were set aflame.

Cries filled the air, those fighting and those dying.

A shudder wracked through her.

Sir William nodded to Kinsey just before they entered the city, indicating here was where she should stay.

Everything in her wanted to keep charging with the men into battle and slay every Englishman she came upon. But she was an archer, a part of Sir William's army, whose deviation could cost Scotsmen their lives.

She reined her horse to a stop and leapt from her steed. The heavy chainmail she wore tugged on her as her feet hit the ground. She wore a blue and red MacLeod tunic belted over the armor, which made her even more ungainly. The horse was battle-trained and remained by her, unflinching amid the clashing metal and screams.

Her hands trembled when she reached for an arrow. Her

fingers swept past the fletching in her haste. She had to get control. She pulled in a slow, careful breath and let it out.

The anxiety racing through her calmed somewhat. Enough to steady her hands. She reached for an arrow, nocked it and gazed through the mass of people to find an English soldier as she'd been instructed.

Black smoke billowed toward her, stinging her eyes and making her throat raw. It limited her visibility, so targets came in flashes and glimpses. Her arm burned from the effort of holding her drawn bow with the weight of chainmail dragging at her. Frustration ground at the base of her neck.

There was not one solitary person she could sight in her aim. There was only chaos.

Blades flashing. People rushing by. Screaming. Blood. And through it all, a thick haze in the air from various huts that had been set aflame.

She searched through it to no avail.

The helm further blocked her sight and the huff of her own breath echoed in her ears. It was impossible to shoot with the damn thing on.

She wrenched the helm off her head. Her renewed senses were brilliantly aware suddenly, like having a candle lit in a dark room. She could see, hear. Focus.

Soldiers in different colored surcoats battled one another, but she wasn't familiar enough to know many of them outside of the red and blue livery of the MacLeod clan. It was those colors she sought.

For if she could find her own army, she could easily find their enemy.

*There.*

A man in chain with a red and blue surcoat was shoved against the wall by a man in a yellow surcoat. Kinsey took aim and released her arrow. A screen of black smoke swept over the scene.

She squinted to see, her heart pounding. Had she hit the Englishman? Or her own man?

The scene reappeared for a blink of a moment. The Englishman lay on the ground with an arrow jutting from his back.

The air whooshed from her lungs with relief.

Her gaze darted through the hellacious scene, seeking out another man from their army to help her identify more English soldiers. On and on she went, repeating the action as she used her fellow soldiers to locate the English guards.

Her arm and back were on fire with exhaustion from drawing her bow repeatedly beneath the weight of the chainmail, but she kept on.

Suddenly, a woman burst from a smoking home, her mouth stretched in a scream, wild with fear. Chills raked down Kinsey's spine and made the hairs along the back of her neck stand on end.

The woman stiffened and pitched forward as her eyes rolled back in her head. She fell into the dirt without ceremony. An axe handle jutted up from her back amid a dark stain of blood.

Kinsey gasped and involuntarily stepped backward.

The soldier behind her was one whose liveries she recognized. White stars on a blue background. One of Sir James's soldiers. One of the men who fought to reclaim land for Scotland.

Bile rose in her throat. He had killed a woman. An unarmed woman. From behind as she ran.

Kinsey shifted her focus, no longer seeking soldiers to hit with her arrows, but searching for the townspeople. A man wearing a tunic and no weapon in his hand was run through with a sword. Another woman running, crying as another soldier chased after her.

This wasn't vengeance.

This was a slaughter.

They were supposed to reclaim land under English rule by fighting soldiers, not by killing unarmed people.

A sudden rush of awareness tingled at the base of Kinsey's neck. She spun about, narrowly missing the thrust of a blade at her back.

"Man or woman makes no difference to me," the soldier wearing white and red livery bellowed as he swung his sword. "Die, Scottish whore."

She leapt out of the way, heavier and more cumbersome in her chainmail. A breeze of air swept past her cheek from the weapon.

It had been close.

Too close.

She reached for an arrow, but before she could nock it, he was charging at her once more. There were only so many times she could evade his sword before her armor would cause her to be too slow.

Her fingers worked blindly over her belt as she spun away, freeing her dagger.

Agony exploded at the back of her head. She tried to jerk away, and the pain worsened. The bastard had her by the hair.

Drake had always taught them how to rush into an attack rather than from it. She did exactly that now, turning suddenly and racing toward the English soldier, her dagger locked tight in her right hand.

The bastard hadn't been expecting the attack and didn't have time to block her as she thrust the dagger up into his neck. Hot blood gushed out of his throat, splashing over her hands and face and soaking into her tunic.

She jerked in surprise, and he dropped to his knees. A strange, awful gargling sound rattled in his throat as bubbles frothed at the blood still gushing from the wound.

Her stomach roiled.

He pitched on his side, his blue eyes fixing first on her in uncomprehending surprise, then on nothing as his body slowly relaxed.

Kinsey couldn't stop staring. He was dead.

*She* had killed him.

She staggered back in horror. His blood stained her hands, creasing in sticky folds at her palms, and the taste of it lingered thick and coppery in her mouth.

Her stomach heaved again, and she retched.

A new cry rose up from the city center, not one of terror or death, but of victory.

They had won.

Why then did it feel more like a defeat?

Wᵢₗₗᵢₐₘ lifted his arms in triumph with his fellow Scotsmen, but he didn't join in their chants. His chainmail was still clean, absent any blood. He hadn't spilled a drop. Not when so many had been unarmed.

Laird MacLeod stood several paces away, near the king, his chest puffed with pride.

How could his father stand it? To be part of a slaughter of merchants and families?

The city had yielded swiftly, the English soldiers and knights keenly aware of their defenses' futility.

William glanced around at his men, confirming all were accounted for. They were. But one particular woman was not.

Reid met his eye and slipped away, apparently being of the same mind and worry for Kinsey. When he returned with her at his side, she was missing her helm and covered in blood. Her fingers clutched her bow with a white-knuckled grip.

Fear stabbed through William. "Have ye been hurt?" he asked in a low voice for her ears only.

"Nay." Her jaw set. "An English soldier attacked me, but I had my dagger."

William looked to Reid, who nodded in confirmation. The soldier was dead. By Kinsey's hand.

Her expression was hard. William knew the look well. It was of a soldier set on ignoring what she'd seen. What she'd done.

She wanted out of here as badly as he did, no doubt.

Mayhap more so.

"I dinna know about the lot of ye," William said to his band of men. "But I could use an ale."

It was as good an excuse as any, and the resounding cheer told him his men were eager to indulge. William jerked his head toward Edinburgh, indicating they should make their way back to the inn. The men didn't need to be told twice.

Kinsey didn't speak to anyone on their journey or upon their arrival at the inn. He hesitated before approaching her. Usually, women liked to talk about their troubles. Some preferred to do as he did, mulling over their thoughts, working at them until the rough edges had been rolled smooth. But Kinsey was different than any other woman he'd ever known, and he wasn't quite sure how to handle her.

He caught her attention before she climbed the stairs to the rented rooms. "Are ye well, Kinsey?"

Her tunic was stained with blood, and crimson dots spotted her face and neck. Her pale blue eyes were wide in her face, her lips tucked against one another tightly. She nodded.

Reid appeared then, looking apologetic. "Laird MacLeod has summoned ye to the castle."

"Aye, in a moment." William knew he probably didn't have even that much time. But his reply was enough to satisfy Reid, who made his way up the stairs to remove his chainmail and wash after the battle.

William wished he could do likewise. His skin was gritty beneath the gambeson that kept the chainmail from chaffing.

He put a hand on Kinsey's shoulder. "If ye dinna want to come to the castle to celebrate later, dinna feel like—"

"I'm well." She gave him a tight smile. "I'll be there."

He hesitated, hating that he had to see his father at the castle. "Until then, my lady." He offered her a bow, and she didn't even bother to roll her eyes.

Aye, she was certainly not well as she claimed.

Back at Edinburgh Castle, his father, as well as other lairds, chieftains and earls, all met with the king in the Great Hall while wearing their battle dress. The king was young, more lad than man at only seventeen.

The high ceiling arched over them all, the thick, heavy beams as decorative as they were functional. The scent of meadowsweet lingered in the air, suggesting the rushes had been changed recently.

King David paced in his royal armor, his surcoat stained with blood and smoke and sweat from leading his men into Lothian. His eyes flashed with excitement as he spoke of their victory and his expectation that the men should be ready to move soon. This time, they'd raid the English territories through Northumberland, before laying siege to Newcastle.

Which left only one day to strategize.

But while all the other men nodded in agreement, William could not stifle his doubt. "We need more than a day to plan."

His father shot him a stern look.

"The English have a new weapon," William continued. "'Tis called the *pot-de-fer*. It can shoot a bolt with such power that it cleaves through men, sometimes two at once."

Several of the men looked askance at one another.

King David regarded William thoughtfully. His chin speckled with the fuzzy hair of adolescence. "Our victory today was almost easy." He smirked. "I appreciate yer consideration but I am confident in my decision. We leave in two days." He nodded with finality. "Prepare yer men."

Everyone seated at the large table rose. William made his way to the exit, eager to return to the inn. Not only to clean the filth of war from his skin and to take off the damnably uncomfortable chainmail but to see to Kinsey. She'd weighed on his thoughts as King David planned their next moves.

"William," Laird MacLeod ground out. "Dinna ever question the king."

William gritted his teeth. "The weapon needs to be taken into consideration. If Mabrick Castle had one—"

"And ye're a skilled enough soldier to offer the king advice?" His father's eyes narrowed. "Ye were defeated. What if he asked ye about that before all these men?"

"Then I'd have answered truthfully. Who better to know what to expect than someone who had failed?" He held his father's gaze, but Laird MacLeod's mouth pulled down in a frown.

Irritation burned through William. He was man enough to realize his mistakes and be better in the future for them. The king was playing a dangerous game, and they were all pawns.

William shoved aside his anger and strode in the opposite direction of his father. The king caught his eye and waved him over with a curl of his finger.

William approached and hoped his annoyance didn't show on his face.

"Sir William, is it?" The king lifted his brows, assuming an air of pretension that looked ridiculous on so young a man.

"Aye, my liege." William folded his arms behind his back.

"I appreciate ye speaking yer mind," the king said. "What do ye know of this weapon?"

"I believe the English are arming their castles with it," William replied. "I canna say how mobile it is, but 'tis far more powerful than anything I've seen before."

King David's eye narrowed as if the concept of such a thing physically pained him. "Yer army knows what to look for with this weapon?"

"Aye, Yer Majesty."

The king touched the side of his forefinger to his chin in

elegant thought. "I want them to ride ahead of our raiding party and report any instances of rumors of this *pot-de-fer* ye say they've encountered before. If they see it, they'll need to return to my army to warn them in advance."

William's men wouldn't need to be involved in the raid. He almost gasped out his breath of relief. "As ye wish, sire."

"Aye, 'tis a sound plan." The king nodded to himself. "Ye may go."

William bowed to the young king and returned to the inn.

His men filled the tables, working through several rounds of ale before the celebration at the castle. They cheered at his arrival, raising their mugs in the air to welcome him.

One face was missing, however.

Reid shook his head, answering William's silent question. Kinsey had not yet been down. William climbed the stairs and paused at her door to gently knock. "Kinsey, are ye well?"

The sound of water sloshing came from the other side of the door. "Aye," she replied. "Why wouldn't I be?"

"Ye've no' come down." He rolled his eyes at himself. He should have just seen to himself and given her more time to clean up. Lasses always took a fair amount of time to ready themselves, especially for a celebration.

No matter how unwarranted it might be.

"I had to take a bath." There was a small splash, confirming her claim.

Images flashed in his mind then. Kinsey naked, flame-red hair trailing down her lithe body, her pale skin slick with scented water. His ballocks tightened, and his cock began to stiffen. He glanced down the hall to confirm he was alone and adjusted himself, a feat not easily done through a heavy surcoat.

He closed his eyes, banishing her wet, naked body from his mind. Whatever she needed right now, it was not lust.

"I had blood in my hair." She said it so quietly, he almost didn't hear her.

That softened his burgeoning arousal. "Do ye need me to send up a maid?"

"Nay." Her voice was tight. "Please leave me be."

William backed away. She needed time. That was something he understood.

He said nothing further, leaving her be as she'd asked. But he vowed that if she did not seem recovered by that evening at the castle, he would not let the matter go.

THE REVELRY IN THE GREAT HALL OF EDINBURGH CASTLE WAS tremendous. The castle was grand with tapestries glittering with gilt thread, merry music played by a small band of musicians and trestles laden with more food than they could possibly eat. Salted pork, roasted pheasant, meat pies, vegetables of all kinds, nuts, cheese and pastries.

And all of it turned dry and tasteless on Kinsey's tongue. She swallowed a mouthful of ale to force a bit of meat pie down her throat.

Duff, who sat to her right and had indulged himself with far too much wine, nudged her elbow. "Eh, Kinsey?"

She smiled so brightly, it exacerbated the hollowness inside her. "Ach, aye," she agreed without knowing what he was asking.

"I told ye." Duff's face lit up, his cheeks flushed from drink and his teeth tinged purple. He slapped his hand on the table and wheezed a laugh.

As soon as the focus was off her, Kinsey dropped the facade and let the smile melt from her lips. She didn't want to be there. But would being in her room be any better?

An image of the tub flashed in her mind, the water red with the blood she'd washed from her hair. From her hands. She looked down at her palms. They were absent any traces of gore. Her fingers, however, contained flecks of it, clinging to the cuticles of her nails. Blood from the man she'd killed. His face lodged stubbornly in her mind.

Those blue eyes, bulging with surprise, his stare slipping into the distance as his life—

Someone plunked down onto the seat at her left. "Are ye enjoying the feast?"

Sir William tossed her one of his charming grins.

She tried to put on a pleasant smile. "Aye."

"How did ye find yer food?"

She slid her gaze to her trencher, where the small amount she'd taken had been pushed around the slab of stale bread until it had begun to soak through. "Delicious."

"Ye enjoyed the two bites ye had?"

She pursed her lips.

He leaned closer, bringing with him that scent that so enticed her, that masculine, warm spice, and spoke in a quiet voice. "Can I be honest with ye?"

He was so near, the heat of his body was evident against her skin. It made her want to nuzzle against the strength of him, to feel his arms embrace her.

She shoved aside that longing. "Of course."

"I dinna care for raids." He frowned. "Too many innocents get hurt."

Kinsey's heart squeezed at the memory of the woman who had been slain. How many unarmed people were killed without thought or mercy?

"I didn't know it would be like that," she admitted.

"I have another confession," he said.

She looked up at him.

"I dinna like this feast." He shook his head, and a lock of dark hair fell over his forehead. He brushed it away thoughtlessly. "I dinna like to celebrate what our king forced us to do."

It wasn't wise to speak ill of their monarch, especially when he was in the same room, no matter how large it might be. But his candor touched the tender, wounded place inside her.

"I can walk ye back to the inn if ye like," he offered.

Normally she would refuse with a curt reply. She would assume he might try to take advantage of their time alone with an eager mouth and hands. She would flash her dagger and remind him how she could care for herself.

Of course, that would have been before he'd kissed her.

Before she craved him.

Before she'd killed a man and so desperately needed to forget.

Right now, she didn't want to be alone. Not at the feast, or on the road walking back, or in her room at the inn, with only a flickering candle to keep away the dark and the press of loneliness.

"The men are too sotted to notice." He glanced around at the men by way of confirming what he'd said.

Duff swayed beside Kinsey, while several others all spoke at once, their words slurred and their faces ruddy with drink.

He was right. They wouldn't notice if she stayed any more than they would notice who she had left with.

She nodded.

Sir William didn't offer a cocky reply or bother with any other form of arrogance. He simply stood and offered her his arm, his expression earnest.

The streets of Edinburgh were crowded with the sort who emerged only at night. Those seeking entertainment, those willing to provide it—in all its forms—and those whose intentions were doubtless nefarious.

Regardless, the night was quiet and cool, a soothing balm to her ragged nerves. And a refreshing contrast from the crowded, overly lit feast that buzzed with noise and blazed with the heat of too many people.

William walked her into the inn, then up the stairs to the rooms, stopping when they arrived at the door before her chamber. The reminder of the bloody tub shot forefront to her mind once more, the water clouded red and her stained clothing balled up beside it.

She didn't want to go inside and face the metallic odor of death.

"Kinsey."

She started at Sir William's voice and looked up into his concerned gaze.

"Would ye rather go downstairs and have an ale first?" he asked.

The thought of being surrounded by people once more made her chest constrict. She shook her head vigorously.

"We could find a quiet corner," he suggested.

There would still be too many people. She wanted quiet. Peace. Would there ever be peace with that tub of soiled water?

"There's blood in my room." She said it so abruptly that she surprised even herself. "I—in the tub. And on my clothes." Bile rose in her throat.

He put his hand to the handle of the door. "May I?"

She gave a terse nod.

He opened the door, went in and quickly shut it before she could see within. Her breath remained locked in her lungs as she waited, her nerves strung tautly. Several minutes later, he opened the door again. "'Tis fine."

She peered inside where a fire had recently been lit, its smoky scent overwhelming the odor of blood. The tub and her clothing were gone. She blinked in wonder and looked at him.

"It wasna me." He indicated the cleared space. "The maids saw to it."

All at once, Kinsey felt like a complete and utter fool for her fears.

"Thank ye," she said. "For opening the door to check. And lighting the fire. Ye must think me daft."

"Nay." He put his hands to her shoulders gently. "Nay. Raids are...difficult. I dinna like them."

"Ye said as much earlier." She studied his handsome face. "Why did ye do it?"

He scoffed. "Our king commanded it of my men and me. I canna decline the king." He struck a bit of flint together and lit a candle by the bed. "I should go."

Her pulse kicked up with a panicked flutter. "Please don't." Her forced smile was tight. She was being ridiculous. "Stay. For just a moment." She searched his eyes, silently imploring him. "Please."

He studied her in quiet consideration, then nodded and shut the door.

She stared hard at the ground before squeezing her eyes closed. "I'd never killed a man before joining ye. It was different at Mabrick Castle when they were far away. But today..."

"I know," he said gently.

She blinked her eyes open and found him opening his arms to her. He didn't come to her, but rather remained in place so that she could accept his offer if she wished.

Without another thought, she rushed into his embrace, and finally yielded to the strength she'd spent the night craving.

## ❧ 12 ❧

**W**illiam held Kinsey as she clung to him. She didn't cry as most women assuredly would have, but he sensed her drawing comfort nonetheless, by the way that her fingers dug into his tunic.

Guilt gnawed at him.

He'd been so preoccupied with finding a good archer to provide him with an upper hand in battle that he hadn't put enough consideration into Kinsey. Aye, he'd wanted her as a man longed for a woman and as a commander needed an archer, but he'd never thought how she might be affected by the killing.

What she had been forced to do for him had shattered something innocent inside her, a piece she would never be able to get back.

She released him and leaned back to look up at him, her gaze sheepishly settling to where her palms rested on his chest still. "Ye must think I'm terribly weak."

He shook his head. "I know how strong ye are. I shouldna have asked ye to join us. I shouldna have exposed ye to war."

Her jaw clenched. "I can handle it."

"I know ye can." He put his hand over hers where it lay

against his chest. "But do ye want to?"

She watched him silently.

"I was so stunned after the first man I killed that I was almost slain myself," he admitted.

She tilted her head at him, and firelight glinted off her glossy red curls. "Ye were?"

"Aye." He allowed himself to recall that awful day on the battlefield, the one he'd pushed away every time it nudged at his conscience. "I ran him through the chest with my sword. I remember every detail about him."

*The gurgle in his chest, the dribbles of blood from his lips that had stained his gray mustache. The way his brown eyes had widened in surprise as if asking how such a thing might have happened.*

"I was so taken aback that I was frozen in place." William shrugged. The simple action indicated the memory didn't matter when they both knew it did. "One of the MacDonalds came up behind me, intending to smash my skull in with a hammer."

Kinsey's brows tensed. "What happened?"

"Reid was there beside me. He killed the man, which brought me back to my senses." A profound sense of gratitude washed over William as he thought about his closest friend. There had been so much more between them in their years of friendship. They'd battled side-by-side, saved one another and traveled most of Scotland together.

William touched a hand to her shoulder. "Killing isna easy. It shouldna be easy. Ye'll remember this for the rest of yer life."

Her blue eyes were fixed on his, luminous and wide. As if she were searching into his soul. She reached up, lightly cupping his face in her hands and rose on her toes to press her mouth to his.

Her lips were warm as they moved over his, tentatively at first, then boldly as her tongue brushed his. A helpless groan rumbled in his chest as he drew her toward him without thought, desperate for the sweetness of her mouth. She tilted her head back to deepen the kiss and slid her hand over his shoulder.

Fire raced through his veins and made his cock swell with insistent need. But even as his hands glided over her waist, doubt edged into his thoughts.

He shouldn't be in her room, and he most certainly shouldn't be kissing her.

She arched her body against him, grinding her pelvis to his arousal. Pleasure tingled through his groin.

Her hands eased over the back of his neck, holding him to her, wanting him with her.

*This.*

This was what he knew about women. Desire. Lust. The euphoria of that slow, sweet burn.

His hands skimmed up her narrow waist to the sides of her breasts. She exhaled a sigh and arched her chest into his waiting palms as his thumbs brushed over the smooth linen of her kirtle, finding the peaks of her nipples.

She sucked in a breath, and he knew he'd found exactly the right spot. He teased the small buds through the fabric until they rose hard and eager under his fingertips. How he wished the linen between them was gone, and it was his tongue touching her silky skin instead.

With one hand still on her breast, he slid the other lower to her bottom, cupping her round, firm arse and pushing her more snugly against his raging need. She cried out as her kisses became more urgent. Her thighs parted around one of his, and she rubbed over him in a desperate rhythm he knew all too well.

Aye, this was what they both needed.

The bed was near. He wanted her underneath him, so they could fit their bodies together properly. So he could ease her neckline down and free her breasts for him to lick and suck and tease.

He lowered both hands to her thighs and pulled, gentle but firm, lifting her onto his hips, where her thighs locked around him.

It would be so easy to shift her skirt aside. She was already spread open for him, and he knew without a doubt that she would be slick with yearning, that he could easily plunge into her.

But, nay, he'd spent too much time waiting for his moment to rush. He wanted to take his time with her.

He carried Kinsey to the bed, braced himself on the coverlet with one arm, and carefully lowered them both to the mattress. Her legs remained spread over his hips, her fingers now freely roaming over his chest, his arms, his stomach.

Her touch brushed over his cock, and he hissed out a breath.

At that point, there was a line drawn, one he knew once crossed would be difficult to turn back. He looked down to gaze at the woman he wanted so badly, the woman he'd been restricted from having.

Aye, she was beautiful, more so than ever before, if such a thing were even possible. Her cheeks were flushed, her hair in wild disarray and her mouth rosy from their frantic kissing. He wanted to make her cry out with pleasure. To sate her in ways she never dreamed.

Then his father's image, of all unwanted things, appeared in William's mind. How Laird MacLeod's mouth had curled around the word "whore."

He drew back.

What was he doing? She was upset over the man she'd slain, over the ugliness of a raid. She needed comfort, not passion.

Kinsey reached for him. "Nay."

He shook his head. "This isna what ye need right now."

"I need to forget." She looked up at him, meeting his gaze with a heavy-lidded stare, her hair flowing in a tangle of curls. "I need ye."

Such exquisite temptation.

"Ye have me," he said, the admission was more sincere than he cared for it to be.

She arched her hips where her thighs still locked around him, so their pelvises ground against one another. Her head dropped back with a moan.

His ballocks tightened with the bliss of that sweet friction. There was, of course, something he could do for her while still ensuring she remained pure.

He moved off of her, and she gave a small whimper of protest. But he didn't leave. Instead, he lay on the bed beside her.

"Lean against me," he said.

The bed creaked on its ropes as she adjusted her position, so she nestled her back against him. She wriggled closer, pressing her round arse against the hardness of his cock. He gritted his teeth and focused his thoughts.

She glanced over her shoulder at him, her expression coy.

This might be the most difficult thing he'd done in his life: to give gratification and not accept it in return.

KINSEY'S MIND SPUN WITH AN INTOXICATING LIGHTNESS, bringing pleasure and frustration alike.

William's body was a wall of strength against her backside. She arched into him, unable to cease the flex of her hips any more than she could snuff the flame of her desire.

When she was kissing William, when his hands were on her, she wasn't thinking of the man she'd killed or the woman who had been slain. There was no missing her family and home or having her heart break just a little more at the loss of Fib. There was nothing but the transcendence of their intimacy.

William brushed her hair over her shoulder. Awareness heightened every one of her senses and the simple touch of her hair sweeping over her skin nearly made her gasp aloud. He wrapped his muscular arm around her, protective, possessive, sensual.

His lips found the back of her neck. His warm mouth, the rasp of his whiskers—her skin prickled with a delicious wave of pleasure. He administered tender, suckling kisses down the slope of her shoulder as he untied the back of her kirtle and lowered her sleeve to expose her shoulder.

Her heart raced with anticipation. She wanted her clothing off faster, and his too for that matter, to experience the press of their nakedness together.

She had never been curious about what went on between a man and a woman. She knew the basic details, of course. She'd seen drunks rutting behind taverns with the wenches who served them their ale. Never before had she wanted it. She did now—with every primal part of her being.

But William didn't strip her clothes off her. Instead, he kissed her exposed shoulder and eased his hand into the neckline of her kirtle. His warm palm found her naked breast beneath as his deft fingers rolled and worked over her nipple until she was crying out.

Slowly, he moved the other breast, repeating the intimate massage as he kissed his way up her neck to her earlobe.

She moaned, panting with need, sounds far too loud in the otherwise quiet room, but she didn't care. Not when her need was so great. She would do anything at that moment to get a release from the building tension at her core.

Anything.

He eased his hand from her breast and shifted outside her kirtle, moving lower, past her navel. Kinsey's heartbeat snagged. Was he going to touch her? *There?*

She parted her knees as his fingers brushed over the juncture between her thighs. Her body jerked instinctively, twitching toward him. His hand curled inward, gliding between her thighs. Her pulse raced with wild delight.

No longer caring about anything but the bliss of his touch, she spread her legs as he rubbed her sex through her clothing.

"I want to bring ye pleasure." His spicy breath was hot against her ear.

She moaned.

He gave a little growl in reply and inched her skirt upward. His arousal pressed against her bottom, heavy with lust. She wanted it thrusting inside her to sate the driving need in her core.

Her hips arched back toward him, grinding him more fully. His hand fisted in the fabric of her skirt before continuing to draw the garment higher. He didn't stop until her legs were bare, and the triangle of red hair between her legs was just barely hidden by the hem.

William's breath came faster in her ear.

"Touch me," she whispered.

He groaned and his feather-light touch inched up her inner thigh to sweep over her sex. Pleasure blossomed between her thighs, making her center burn hotter, pulse deeper.

He gave a low curse. "Ye're so wet," he said hoarsely.

His finger stroked over her again, more firmly, toward a place so sensitive, she immediately cried out.

"Aye, there." His teeth gently caught her earlobe, his breath heavy in her ear. "Ye like that?"

"Aye," she gasped.

His digit circled the spot, and her frantic breath became husky with moans. Just when she thought she might die from the intensity of it, his hand slid lower, and something carefully nudged inside her.

It was so close to the fire burning inside her. A tease, really. She needed more. Her hips arched upward to encourage him deeper. His shoulder shifted against hers as he repositioned his hand.

His finger eased into her as he also rubbed at the sensitive place above her sex. "Like this?" he murmured.

She spread her thighs wider, moving her hips in time with the careful pumping of his hand. Pleasure was everywhere. Building inside her. Pounding through her blood. Tightening into a brilliant ball that would soon shatter. She couldn't even speak to reply.

He kissed her below her ear, his breath as frantic as hers. "Come for me, lass," he ground out in a thick Scottish burr. "I want to hear ye cry out with yer release."

His ministrations quickened, his hand almost vibrating against her. Too much. All of it.

Her body tensed.

He growled in her ear, and it was her undoing. Euphoria exploded somewhere inside her, clenching around his finger as he continued to thrust it into her. She clung to his arm and squeezed her thighs against his hand.

It might have lasted for a second or a lifetime, she couldn't tell, but when she finally floated down from the heaven she'd been sent to, she was depleted of energy. Her thighs dropped, and she sagged back against William, his arousal still rock hard at her back.

He kissed the spot below her ear, just behind her jaw. "That was beautiful." He brushed a strand of hair from her face and tucked it back. "God, ye're the bonniest lass I've ever laid eyes on."

A languid smile curled over her lips. "Ye needn't flatter me." She rolled toward him without bothering to cover her exposed lower half. "I want this." Her gaze held his as her fingers trailed over his strong chest, down the bands of muscle at his abdomen, discernible even through the linen of his leine. She framed the column of his ready prick with her hand. "I want ye."

His eyes closed. He drew in a deep breath before opening them again. "Nay, lass. That was for ye."

There was a place deep inside her that didn't want his refusal, something that needed the rest of him.

But he plucked her hand gently from his body. "Ye need rest."

She opened her mouth to protest, but he leveled a stern look at her. "I believe ye said ye wanted to be a warrior and no' a leman."

Heat touched her face.

"And a warrior follows instructions," he continued. "Right now, ye need rest."

She didn't want to go to sleep. Nay, that wasn't completely true. Her body was heavy and liquid. If her eyes fell closed, slumber would easily carry her away.

She didn't want him to go.

"Please don't leave me," she said.

"Ye're an obstinate warrior," he said with mock chastisement.

"Ye like that about me."

He grinned. "Aye, I do." His gaze skimmed down her face, then back up. "But I canna have ye seducing me."

A smile pulled at her lips. "If I promise not to?"

He issued forth a dramatic sigh. "Verra well. If ye turn round and go to sleep, I'll stay with ye tonight."

She glanced down once more where his prick strained against his trews and pursed her lips with regret. After all, her maidenhead was of little consequence. She didn't anticipate a noble match as her sister Faye's had been.

Kinsey didn't want marriage or children or anything having to do with the lot of it. What she did with her maidenhead would be her own decision.

She turned away from him, and his arm fell over her once more, warm and protective.

"Sleep well, my lass," he whispered in her ear.

In all honesty, she'd meant to break her promise. Her intention had been to stay awake until he slept, then nudge back against the thickness of his arousal jutting at her bottom.

Except in the time that she waited for him, locked in the safety of his embrace, sated by the intimacy they'd shared, the pull of sleep was more than she could resist.

It would have to be morning then when she broke her promise. As she fully intended to do.

## ❧ 13 ❧

**W**illiam had difficulty sleeping through the night. Not because he was uncomfortable, but quite the opposite.

Kinsey slept soundly in his arms, her face relaxed in peace, beautiful and still with only the steady rise and fall of her lovely bosom. Her hair splashed over the pillow like silken fire, and she was warm where she fit perfectly against him, their bodies cradled together.

He seldom fell asleep with women and never like this, never with her nestled against him. It gave him a sense of vulnerability. Not only him, but both of them.

She trusted him.

Mayhap that trust was part of the reason he kept sleep at bay. He wanted to ensure he woke early enough that no one would see him leave her room. He would have no one thinking ill of her for their time together, not when the night had been so poignant.

It was with great reluctance that he finally pulled his arm free from where it curled against her. He rose carefully from the bed, so as not to disturb her. Kinsey pouted in her sleep, giving a little whimper of protest as she reached for him.

God, how he wanted to kiss the softness of her sleep-warm skin, to hold her in his arms and stay with her all morning. Memories of her coming undone as he brought her to climax echoed in his mind. It had been exquisite to see her pleasure, to drink it in as his own. How he longed to hear such sounds again soon, to give her such enjoyment.

But not now.

He glanced at her on the bed one final time and slipped regretfully from her room. The dim light of the hall was dove gray with the dawn of a new day. The chill in the air was a startling contrast from the warmth of the bed they'd shared.

A figure moved down the hall.

William tensed, immediately on high alert.

Reid stepped from the shadows. Damn him for always getting up too bloody early.

He glanced at Kinsey's door and lifted a brow.

William frowned at his friend and shook his head to indicate he hadn't lain with Kinsey, as least, not in the way obviously expected.

Reid's other brow raised as well, so they both were flexed upward in surprise.

William smirked and returned to his own room to make ready for the day ahead. There would be many preparations to get underway before leaving the following morning for Newcastle upon Tyne, where the king intended to lay siege. At least William's army wouldn't be involved in the raids leading up to it.

A shiver of apprehension wound down his spine.

That apprehension was only further exacerbated when William met with his father that morning and was informed that they would be leaving for Newcastle immediately with the overeager king and several other trusted men.

There was only time to pack and give final orders to Reid quickly. William summoned his friend to his room while he assembled his belongings.

"I'll ensure we arrive posthaste," Reid said sincerely.

"I dinna doubt it." William tossed his friend a grateful smile and reached for a stack of freshly laundered leines, thanks to the maids of the tavern.

Reid folded his arms and watched as William shoved the rest of his clothes into a wax-sealed sack. "Did ye hear how Edinburgh Castle was reclaimed?"

William paused in his task, searching his memory. "By Sir William Douglas, aye?"

"Aye, but did ye hear how?"

William shook his head and surveyed the small room one final time to ensure he hadn't forgotten anything. Not that it seemed likely, when there was little more to the room than a bed, a table with an ewer and a shuttered window.

"Sir William and his men dressed as merchants hauling hay into the castle," Reid explained. "Once they were allowed inside, they leapt from the wagon and took the castle."

William went still. "Mabrick."

Reid nodded slowly. "'Twas my first thought too. I knew it'd be yers as well."

The hardest part of taking a castle was breaching the walls. If they could get inside, William had enough confidence in his men to know they could overpower the Englishmen.

"Newcastle is only two days ride from Mabrick," William said to himself.

Reid gave a rare smile, evidently well aware of this fact.

William slapped him on the shoulder. "Nicely done."

"Best be offering yer farewells. At least to one soldier in particular." Reid winked and slipped from the room.

William chuckled, knowing exactly who Reid referred to. And indeed, William had made sure to spare a moment to at least offer Kinsey a farewell.

He cinched up the pack, tying it tightly so nothing gaped open. No doubt, there would be rain along the way, and there was nothing worse than wet clothing upon arriving at a camp where nothing ever dried out properly.

He opened the door and stepped out into the hall, already anticipating seeing Kinsey. Except that his father stood several paces away, arms folded casually over his chest as he waited.

There would be no getting around him to go to Kinsey, and William refused to go to her with his da present.

Laird MacLeod noticed William and approached. "Come, lad. The horses are waiting."

William didn't so much as glance at Kinsey's door as he passed. Still, something squeezed in his chest. He hated leaving like this after what they'd shared the evening before.

The journey to Newcastle would take four days, and with William a day ahead, he would not see her for five at least.

He and his father strode from the inn into the drizzling rain. The heavy clouds overhead promised even more rain as the day pressed on. The stable lad took William's pack and secured it to the horse alongside a bit of food and a bedroll.

"Ye've done well, William." His father climbed onto his own steed.

William mounted his horse and regarded Laird MacLeod with a careful look, unsure if he'd heard correctly, but almost afraid to ask.

His father shook his head with a laugh. "Aye, ye heard me right, lad." He clicked his tongue, and their horses began to climb the steep street toward the castle where the others were waiting. "Yer army is well trained. I see how they listen to ye, and I've witnessed their skill." He nodded in approval. "Ye're a good leader."

Warmth expanded in William's chest, unwanted but glorious regardless. He was a grown man, one whose concern should extend beyond his father's opinion. But those words, small and freely given by others, were ones he'd waited his whole life to hear. A goal finally attained.

"Good enough to lead the clan?" William asked.

His father grinned at him, an older version of William's own smile. It bolstered William's spirits. At least, until Laird MacLeod spoke. "That depends on what marriage ye're considering."

"Marriage?" William shook his head. "It doesna suit me."

They were near to the castle now, where the king and a group of his men gathered for departure.

Laird MacLeod slowed his horse to delay their arrival. "It suits a laird." A frown tugged at his face. "This is what I meant when I said ye were no' ready to be a laird. Ye dinna think of yer people. Ye think of yerself. Ye need only wed a bride. Once ye've secured the marriage, ye can carry on rutting every lass in Christendom."

Such a thought was even worse than marriage to a woman William didn't want.

He'd bedded women married to men who hadn't cared for them, men who were off with other women while William pleased their wives. He'd vowed never to be one of those men.

"The Campbells have a daughter," his father continued. "She's bonny enough. She hasna much wit about her, but her dowry will bring land and a considerable fortune. It would secure our alliance with the clan, which would be a great benefit to yer people."

The Campbells would be a powerful ally, and alliances through marriage were well-sealed. William clenched his jaw, hating the truth behind his father's words.

They were close enough to the others to make out the murmured hum of the men conversing as they mounted their horses for the journey.

"I saw ye last night," Laird MacLeod said abruptly.

William glared at his father. "What do ye mean?"

"With yer archer." His father stopped his horse, forcing William to do likewise. "I'm sure that sharp tongue tasted sweet once ye finally got it tamed." His da winked.

Anger flashed hot in William's chest. "I dinna—"

"Dally with her as ye like." Laird MacLeod narrowed his gray eyes. "But a laird marries for the betterment of his clan. No' his cock."

He turned away without giving William a chance to protest and joined the others.

*Marriage.*

William's chest squeezed at the very idea. The relationship between him and Kinsey was a delicate, fragile thing, slowly growing into something beautiful. Even still, it was far too soon to propose marriage. And even if she did agree to marry him, would his people accept a woman with English blood in her veins?

All at once, he was glad he had not lain with Kinsey despite the temptation and knew he would do well to remember the reality of what his clan needed from him going forward. No matter how much it hurt.

※

KINSEY WOKE LATER THAT MORNING THAN USUAL. HER SLEEP had been deep, her body more rested than it had been in some time.

Before she blinked her eyes open, the reason why rushed back at her. The battle the day before, the horrors of what she'd seen. How William had comforted her.

A sudden thought struck her. She'd begged him to stay with her. He was still there.

She winced inwardly, squeezing her eyes shut, thoroughly humiliated at her memories. The way she'd spread her legs for him, cried out in pleasure, begging him to take her completely. A warm tingle pulsed between her legs. His touch on her had been exquisite.

It had been different then under the cover of night, her mind swimming with terrible images she wanted to forget, when she'd been so overwhelmed with lust. Though she didn't know what embarrassed her more, how she'd reacted to her need, or that he'd rejected her when she'd offered herself to him.

But she wasn't the kind of person to hide from anything. No matter how she had acted, it was better to face William. She opened her eyes and rolled to the other side of the mattress. Her bed was empty, and she suddenly felt all the more foolish.

He had left.

She roused herself, knowing there would be practice to attend soon. And she was a warrior—not some foolish girl losing her head over a man.

She quickly washed and dressed and rushed to the castle, her heart thundering at the idea of seeing William. How would he react? What should she say?

Suddenly, she was grateful for the years she'd left her life uncomplicated by the tangles of men and lust and love. The twisting of her stomach and crowding of her thoughts, all rife with anxiety—it was wretched.

In the end, she didn't have to worry about an encounter with William. He wasn't there at all. Him or his awful father.

She shuddered at how Laird MacLeod's proposition had slithered over her, offering her a few coins for several nights in his bed.

Even with the MacLeod men blessedly absent, the practice was not a good one. Her mind was too fogged with William; her body flitting between mortification and desire. When they were finally dismissed, she brought the hay bale target forward to return it with the rest of their supplies.

Reid was there, putting away his own blunted practice sword.

She nodded at him, and he returned the gesture.

Then she hesitated.

Reid cast her a wary look. "Did ye need something?"

"I…" Her tongue couldn't put together the jumble of questions that were flying around too quickly in her mind. She paused a moment to gather her wits. "Have ye seen Sir William?"

Confusion furrowed Reid's brows. "He left this morning for Newcastle."

His words struck her, taking her aback. William had left and hadn't even bothered to bid her farewell? Nor had he taken the time to mention it the night before. With everything they had shared, how had he concealed that?

"He dinna see ye?" Reid asked.

Kinsey shook her head.

"He told me he was going to." Reid turned away from her to toss several daggers into a sack. "I imagine he had a good reason no' to."

She should walk away, leave this be and discuss it with William when she next saw him.

"What was he going to say?" she pressed.

"Farewell." Reid straightened and narrowed his hazel eyes at her. "He's quite fond of ye, Kinsey. Ye need no' have doubt."

Heat warmed over her, more excited than she wanted to admit. Reid tucked aside the bag of daggers and regarded her with a curious expression as if he were considering saying something.

Her curiosity piqued. "What is it?"

In all the time Kinsey had been with Sir William's army, never once had she seen Reid appear anything less than confident.

"I need to ask ye something." He glanced around and took a step closer.

It was Kinsey's turn to be wary. "What do ye need to ask me?"

He leaned a little closer. "The woman ye were with at the market in Castleton. The dark-haired one."

"Clara?"

"Clara." A single corner of his mouth lifted.

"Aye, she's my sister." Kinsey put a hand on her hip. "What of her?"

He shook his head. "'Tis nothing."

Kinsey tried to study him, but he kept his gaze downcast. "Did ye think her bonny?"

"I imagine all men do." He smirked and strode away.

"She's not married."

He glanced back at her, and a slow grin spread over his face.

Kinsey almost laughed. Reid and Clara, a fierce warrior and a healer. Wouldn't that be a thing?

But then, she was already somewhat giddy by what Reid had said of William. He was quite fond of her.

Enough to give her pleasure without taking it for himself. Enough to nestle her in his arms all night. Enough to have intended to come to her before he left.

And Kinsey, who had never bothered to consider the possibility of love, did not even try to resist the pull of affection toward William. She let herself get swept up in the current of her thoughts and memories of his handsome smile, the way he'd winked at her playfully and how it had made her heart skip a beat.

They left the following morning with instructions to seek out any sign of the *pot-de-fer* as they made their way to Newcastle over the next four days. November's chill edged into the air, carrying with it heavy clouds and rain. In truth, it was an uncomfortable journey, wet and cold.

Still, it was far better than being with the rest of the king's army. They had been told they were all raiding through villages on their way to Newcastle. As they traveled, they encountered evidence of the destruction. It hung in the distance in thick, black clouds and seasoned the air with a smoky odor.

She passed the time with thoughts of William. After all, it was far better to fix her mind on him than allow her thoughts to drift to loneliness and mourning.

She wanted to lose herself in William again, in the passion they'd shared. How she longed for her body to blaze with need, for the insistent thrum between her legs to be sated.

It seemed to take an age for Newcastle to appear before them finally, a stone wall running around the perimeter of the town, encompassing occupants, huts and castle alike. On their journey, they'd seen no evidence of the *pot-de-fer* in the villages they passed. Thanks be to God.

The lawn and forest around the outside of the Newcastle were already dotted with tents where the king and his commanders had set up camp as they waited for their armies to arrive.

The red and blue MacLeod flag caught in the wind, where it whipped and curled. Kinsey's breath quickened with excitement. She'd spent far too much time thinking of William, and now, she was here, ready to see him once more.

Aye, she'd always been impulsive, acting on what she wanted without consideration.

And, oh, how she wanted William.

He emerged from the tent, his square shoulders broader than she remembered, the sweep of his dark hair over his brow far more enticing. He flashed a wide grin at them all and ran toward them.

Toward her.

Finally, she would see him again. Finally, they could be together.

The wait was over.

## ❧ 14 ❧

**W**illiam rushed out to welcome his army as they arrived. Without meaning to, his gaze searched the sea of familiar faces for the vivid splash of red hair.

It was an easy find. His gaze fixed on Kinsey, and his heart stuttered in his chest.

She rode tall and proud on her horse; her chin notched slightly upward as if beckoning him. Her eyes shone a brilliant blue against the gray skies in the distance. She was even bonnier than he'd recalled.

Their last conversation had been in a room where the air held the scent of intimacy, and her sensual cries still rang out in his head. He forced himself to meet with Reid first as his friend leapt off his horse and approached.

William clasped Reid's forearm. "Was yer journey uneventful?"

"As easy as it can be in the mud and rain. And far more uneventful than those villages that were set upon." His gaze ran over the heavily fortified stone wall and spoke quietly. "Do ye think 'tis possible to make Newcastle fall?"

"Depends on how long they can last inside without supplies."

Reid grunted, an unintelligible sound that was answer enough:

he didn't think it possible. At least he was smart enough not to voice his opinion. One never knew who was listening with so many of the king's men surrounding them.

The king's decision to lay siege on Newcastle was overzealous.

William greeted several of his men before stopping in front of Kinsey as she dismounted from her steed. Her slender legs were encased in a pair of trews that hugged her thighs distractingly and a leine that was nipped in at the waist with a belt.

The wind blew at her back, tossing her red curls about her and bringing her sweet perfume toward him. Images flashed in his mind of touching her, kissing her. Every sensation in his body ignited.

His cock stirred.

They could have a dalliance, of course. One that might fade to nothing between now and the time he would have to wed the Campbell lass.

And yet, he couldn't bring himself to have her when he was so well aware of his obligation. His decision to keep his distance from her had been so much easier when she'd been a day behind him in their travel. Seeing her now, however, and being slammed with the memories of the intimacy they'd shared, he wondered if the lairdship was even worthwhile.

"William." His name on her lips made an invisible band around his chest squeeze even tighter.

Best to do it now than before it was too late. Before it would be impossible.

"I need to speak with ye," he said.

"Oh?" She slid him a coy glance that shot straight to his prick. "I need to speak with ye too." She took a step closer. "Alone?"

He swallowed. "Aye. Set up yer tent and then come see me."

Her lips quirked in a sensual smile, and she turned away. He followed her departure, unable to stop himself from watching her round bottom sway side to side in the those tight trews.

*Jesu.*

Guilt sliced through his interest like a blade.

She couldn't be his.

He went back to his tent to wait for her. Time ticked by at an interminable pace as he went over his speech in his head, anticipating how she might reply and what he could say in return. And through it all, he couldn't help but question his decision to become laird.

But could he really choose a woman he'd only known the short side of a month over his people, his birthright? Over what he'd spent a lifetime trying to be worthy of?

The flap to his tent swept inward, and Kinsey was there, wearing those damn trews. She pushed her curls back from her face and sauntered toward him.

"What do ye think?" Her hands skimmed up the sides of her thighs and stopped at her hips, framing them. With a wicked grin, she turned her backside to him and glanced over her shoulder.

The leather fit her curves perfectly.

His mouth went dry.

What did he think?

That he wanted to cup that firm arse in his palms while grinding their bodies together. That he could still edge his fingers into the fitted garment until she was wet beneath his touch and crying out like before.

Only this time, he wouldn't stop.

"'Tis far easier to fight in." She turned back around and kicked a single leg upward in demonstration. Her smile wavered. "Ye don't like it?"

He shook his head. "It isna that." He let his appreciation show as he ogled her from her top to bottom and back again. "I like it verra much."

The air in the small tent warmed, as though heated by the sudden intimacy charging between them.

"I've been looking forward to seeing ye." She stepped closer and gazed up at him. "I've been thinking of ye." Her cheeks flushed with a delicate pink. "Of the last time we were together."

The sweet, delicate scent that he loved so much teased at his senses.

"I'm sorry I left so abruptly," he said. "I meant to bid ye farewell."

"Reid told me." She set her hand on William's chest and slowly drew it upward. A caress. One of intent.

His cock went immediately hard.

*Damn it.*

"He also said ye were quite fond of me." She brushed her body against his and gasped, glancing down at his evident arousal.

"Kinsey." Her name came out as a groan.

She ran her hand down his torso. "William," she purred.

Her eyes were heavy-lidded, sensual. It would be so easy to curl his arms around her slender frame, to pull her close and let the passion between them flare mindlessly out of control.

"We canna do this," he ground out.

She rose on her toes and pressed her hot mouth to his neck. "Tonight," she breathed.

He closed his eyes against the exquisite torment of his need. "Nay." He stepped back from her, and his heel bumped the wall of the tent.

She gave a little laugh even as her brow furrowed with her confusion. "William, what is this about? I thought..." Her confidence faltered. "I thought ye wanted me. I thought we wanted each other."

He ought to lie and tell her he did not but couldn't bring himself to say such a falsehood. Not about this. She deserved to know the truth.

"I do want ye," he admitted. "I want ye so bad I canna sleep at night for thinking of ye."

"Is it because I told ye I didn't want to be yer leman?" She stepped closer. "I don't want to be a leman. I enjoy being a warrior, but we could still be together. And if we are discreet, no one will ever know."

She reached for him, but he shook his head. Her hand paused midair, and her fingers curled inward to the safety of her palm as her arm lowered.

"It isna that." He sighed. "I have to wed. Someone who will help my clan."

Her stare hardened. "Is this where ye ask me to be yer mistress?"

"Nay," he replied vehemently. "I wouldna ever ask that of ye. Nor can I allow what is happening between us to go on knowing I couldna give ye all of me, that I would eventually have to take a wife."

"Eventually," she repeated. "But not now?"

He nodded.

"What if it is years away?" she asked. "Will ye live like a monk?"

"I dinna think I'm the monk type." He tried to give a smile, but it broke under the weight of his responsibility.

"So ye would find others to slake yer lust..." She swallowed and looked angrily away. "But not me?"

The pain in his chest burned like the heart of a fire, and her words were the air blowing upon it, making it glow with heat.

"I canna trust myself with ye," he said.

She lifted her head. "I don't know what that means."

He took her face in his hands, marveling at the silkiness of her skin, the fierce determination glittering in her lovely pale blue eyes and that sweet, sweet scent he wanted to lose himself in. He memorized every delicate freckle that dotted the bridge of her nose and the shape of her delicious mouth.

"I dinna think I could have ye without losing my heart," he admitted.

Tears swelled in her eyes. "So ye'd rather not have me at all?"

"I'm so sorry, my Kinsey." He brushed his thumb over her chin. "I'm so sorry."

"I'm not *yer* Kinsey." She stepped away, withdrawing from his touch, then stiffly turned from him and departed his tent.

He released a long, slow exhale, not that it made him feel a bit better.

There.

It was done.

Except even if it was the right thing to do, it felt so horribly wrong. The ache in his chest widened, splitting into a chasm in his heart.

He had lost Kinsey forever.

༺ৡ༻

SIEGES PROVED TO BE EXCEEDINGLY DULL. ONE HAD LITTLE TO do but sit and wait. And think.

The latter was what brought Kinsey the greatest torment. The thinking.

Her mind tangled with her heart and somehow left her stomach twisting with an anxious unease she did not like. It took the flavor from food and stretched minutes into hours. Nothing could abate the ache lodged in her chest.

In the drag of days that followed, the remainder of the king's armies slowly trickled in after having many successful raids. Their stories left a foul taste in her mouth, and she turned a deaf ear to them, preferring her own company or that of the men of her own army.

Her melancholy only grew worse, no matter how much she tried to force herself to distraction. She practiced archery but found her mind still prodding at the wound of rejection. She'd even tried her hand at learning how to fight with a sword, a poor decision if ever there was one, for it attracted William's attention.

He watched her as she swung the ungainly weapon, sweat

damp on her brow despite the November chill. They all repeated the same lunge and thrust move over and over, but his focus remained locked on her. At least, until he strode toward the group, heading directly for her.

The slam of her heart echoed in her ears and practically rattled her ribs. Not that she gave him any indication she'd even noticed him.

She continued on as if he didn't exist, as if he were not shattering her entire world with his impending presence. Her hands locked more tightly on the hilt in an attempt to still their trembling, and her gaze trained on an invisible enemy.

"Ye're using too much force," he said.

She steeled herself for his presence and turned to face him. The pain in her chest squeezed into an agony that almost robbed her of breath.

She tilted her head at an angle, feigning a disinterest she did not think she could ever feel. "I beg yer pardon?"

"If ye fight against the weight, ye'll tire too quickly." He withdrew his sword as though it weighed nothing. "Use the heft of the blade to help yer attack."

His blade swooped through the air, sailing downward with ease. During practice, he'd pushed up his sleeves, and the muscles along his forearms flexed beneath his sun-golden skin. Powerful, masculine strength that had once held her through the night, which had once so lovingly touched her in the most intimate places.

She shoved the thought violently away, but its sting was not as easily removed.

Mimicking his motions, she swung the blade up and let its bulk drag it downward.

He nodded. "Aye. 'Tis much better. This time, tighten yer grip on yer hilt." He lifted his weapon in demonstration.

She tried to copy him, but he shook his head.

"May I?" He stepped closer, and all the air around Kinsey sucked away, leaving her head spinning.

If she declined, he would know the emotions roiling inside her. Despite her desire not to, she nodded her head.

He came behind her, and that familiar, spicy scent of him splashed over the wound inside her chest like the sharpest vinegar. His hands reached over hers, repositioning them on the hilt.

Mayhap it was her imagination, but his touch was tender. The way it had been under different circumstances.

He spoke as he instructed her, but she did not hear his words. Instead, their conversation played out in her mind.

*I canna trust myself with ye.*

*I dinna think I could have ye without losing my heart.*

A knot swelled at the back of her throat.

"Kinsey."

She looked up at him and wished she hadn't. Their gazes met and held. A flash of pain showed in the depths of his brown eyes. She wanted to be uncaring, but in that moment, a tingle of warmth at her eyes told her she was on the verge of crying.

His hands still covered hers, as if he were hesitant to release her.

A muscle worked in his jaw dark with whiskers, as if he had not shaved in several days, and made her crave the rasp of the bristled hair against her palm. Or the contrast of the smoothness of his lips over hers with the roughness of his chin.

He glanced around, then edged closer, speaking low. "I'm sorry." He paused as though collecting his thoughts. "I..." Whatever he intended to say tapered off.

It was for the best. Hearing it would do her no good.

Nothing he could say would change matters.

She glared at him and jerked her hands from beneath his, allowing rage to blanket her hurt. "I understand the hold on the sword now."

He stepped back with a nod and strode away.

Though she'd wanted him gone, she hated every step that took him farther from her. She craved his warmth, his scent, his touch, even as she wished she'd never known any of them.

What was more, he'd spoke of needing a woman who could offer something to his people. His da was a laird, but Kinsey's grandda was a chieftain.

The Ross Chieftain was a cruel bastard who had stolen her eldest sister from their home and forced her to marry. The union worked out well for Faye, aye, but it didn't excuse what he had done. Kinsey loathed the old man and would rather die than ask him for anything. Even a dowry.

Nor did she want a husband who would only wed her for what she brought him. She would not buy marriage.

Not even for Sir William MacLeod.

## ❧ 15 ❧

It had been a mistake for William to go to Kinsey. Aye, he'd wanted to ensure she was performing the move correctly. But that wasn't the only reason.

She'd been so damn indifferent. Every time they passed, she looked through him as if he didn't exist. He'd tried speaking to her, but she'd just answered as a warrior, the coolness in her blue eyes giving away nothing.

He missed her.

The admission had almost slipped out of his mouth, but he'd just managed to stop himself. He'd caused her enough pain.

For she hadn't been able to hide it all from him. In a flash of a moment, he'd seen it—the hurt swimming in her eyes. Except it hadn't made him feel better, damn it. Knowing her suffering only made him feel worse.

He had done that to her.

It wasn't fair for him to go to her. It had been selfish, and he vowed never to do such again. His communication with her would go through Reid going forward so that William could maintain his distance.

A shout rose somewhere on the field, back near the tree line, followed by the clang of metal. William didn't bother to turn in the direction of the scuffle.

Fights between the men happened more often now as the siege wore on. The soldiers were bored, and disputes among them were common. An arrow sank into the grass near William's feet.

*Kinsey?*

He spun around, fully expecting to face her wrath, but instead discovered an army rushing from the forest and King David's men locked in combat at the perimeter.

William's gaze cut through the battle waging around them, seeking out the brilliance of Kinsey's red hair. He spotted her between two men who raced toward her with blades drawn. She held her sword as William had shown her while she backed up, her stare flitting between her attackers.

Though she wasn't terribly far away, a cluster of Englishmen was racing toward William with intent.

He didn't even think as he charged toward them while trying to keep part of his focus locked on Kinsey. His blade sliced through the first man who met him.

Several feet away, Kinsey blocked a blow, then barely managed to evade the next. William roared with indignation and whipped his blade with fury, connecting to an Englishman's tender neck and then into the eye slit of another man's helm.

All around him, Scotsmen were being slain. Most were not armed for combat. Some had their gambesons on. Precious few actually wore full chainmail or their helms. Winning would be impossible.

He thrust his blade into a final opponent and was able to rush the short distance to Kinsey.

William ran through the man attacking her with a savage growl and jerked his weapon free. "Were ye injured?"

She threw down the dulled practice sword she'd been using and snatched up her bow and quiver. "Nay."

"This is an ambush we were no' ready for." Even as he spoke, three more men ran toward them.

She sent her arrows streaking through the field toward the men charging at them. One was struck in the shoulder, which did little to slow him down, while another fell with an arrow jutting from his helm.

William lifted his sword, preparing to strike the third, who was thus far uninjured. "Ye need to flee, Kinsey."

"I'll not leave ye or the other men here." Another arrow flew at the third man, taking him down as well. "Not when I can help."

"Then fire yer arrows from the trees, but no' here." He ran toward the man with the shoulder wound to keep him from Kinsey. They met in a harsh ring of metal on metal as their blades caught.

William shoved the bastard back to ensure he remained away from Kinsey.

She could fight, aye, but he didn't want her to. Not when she might be injured. Or worse.

Energy exploded in William, swelling with the need to protect. He struck at the man, again and again, raining down blows faster than the man could defend. While William couldn't cut him through the chainmail, the hits would still cause injury.

Any discomfort William could cause would be a benefit. For his part, he was wearing only his gambeson in place of his chainmail. While he could move faster and was less encumbered, he was also vulnerable.

His opponent staggered back, and William didn't hesitate to end their battle with a lethal strike.

He spun around, but Kinsey wasn't where he'd left her.

*Damn.*

He knew better than to assume she'd listened to him and gone to the forest. Reid was several feet away, fighting off five other men. An unfair number. William raced to his side, letting his blade join that of his friend's.

"Get the men and meet in the forest," William said. There had been a predetermined place named in the thick woods, near where a collection of large stones by the river created a cave-like hollow for them to hide within. A meeting place was something William had always named prior to any battle or siege in his refusal to lose any more men than was necessary.

"I was hoping ye'd say that." Reid plunged his blade into an Englishman to his right.

Once their attackers had been defeated, he and Reid separated to gather the men. William ran through the field, minding the bodies underfoot, his attention on full alert for any danger as he found his men and directed them to meet in the forest. His peripheral trained for the sight of a flash of red hair.

A clang of weapons called his attention. He glanced up and froze.

Kinsey had somehow procured a sword again and was arcing the blade as William had shown her, blocking an Englishman's battle axe from slamming into her head. She wore no helmet, only her trews and the leine with the leather belt at her waist. Her hair had been bound back in a braid, but in combat had come loose, flying in streams of vivid curls around her.

He dashed toward her, but something slammed hard into his back, sending him sprawling on the ground. His lungs seemed to suck in on themselves, not allowing air into his chest. He pushed upright and choked in a breath as a massive hammer flew toward his torso.

His body shifted to the left before his mind could catch up. But once the wind of the hammer's missed strike blew past him, he'd recovered from the hearty blow and charged toward his new opponent. William shoved into the man's abdomen, not stopping until the Englishman's feet were skittering over the ground, and he toppled backward with William atop him.

The man had a mail coif beneath his helm. William growled his frustration. He'd wanted to slay the man and return to Kinsey.

If he was not already too late.

*Nay.*

He shoved at the man's helm, knocking it from his head. Wide green eyes blinked up at him as the Englishman was momentarily stunned by the sun. In that brief moment, William was able to yank the coif from the man's head, revealing his vulnerable neck.

The Englishman snarled in outrage and swung toward William, catching him in the side where he'd been struck by an arrow three weeks earlier. Pain exploded at the old wound he'd thought fully healed, and his body locked up around the agony.

William's world spun around him as he was rolled over onto his back. He closed his hand around his sword and found no hilt in his palm. Somehow, he had dropped his sword.

A metallic taste filled his mouth.

Fear.

The Englishman rose over him, pinning him into place, lifting the hammer high overhead. William struggled against the man's weight as his opponent grinned at his impending victory.

William's mind raced with ways he might free himself, all futile. And with thoughts of Kinsey.

He would not be able to save her.

❦

KINSEY GRABBED UP THE BOW FROM THE GROUND WHERE IT had fallen when she'd picked up the discarded sword. Urgency blared in her head like a scream. There wasn't a second to spare. She grabbed an arrow from the quiver where it still lay in the grass, nocking it as she straightened.

There was no time to think, to breathe. There wasn't even a moment for her hands to tremble with the rapid firing of her pulse. She loosed the arrow. It flew through the air toward the man hefting the hammer over William.

Her heart snagged mid-beat, and for one instant, everything froze.

If she missed...

The arrow sank into the back of the man's neck.

The Englishman sagged to his side, the hammer tumbling harmlessly to the ground.

Kinsey's gasped out an exhale at her incredible luck. She lifted her quiver to her back, along with her bow, with hands that did shake now. And badly.

She left the sword where she had dropped it. There were many scattered on the field beside dead men. Far too many of them were Scots.

William's lesson about using the weapon's weight rather than fighting it had saved her life. And allowed her to save his.

She ran toward William as he shoved the Englishman off him and staggered to his feet, dragging his sword with him.

Blood flecked his face and gambeson, his hair disheveled from the struggle. But he was alive.

Hysteria tickled at the back of her throat, and her eyes swam with tears. She wanted to laugh. To cry. To do both at once and neither at all.

He was alive.

He met her halfway as his gaze skimmed the area around them. "We need to go to the forest. The men have been told already." A sense of urgency rushed his words.

She knew what he saw, what had put the authoritative finality to his voice. Scotsmen lay dead in the fields they had once hoped to reclaim. Slaughtered without armor, some without even weapons.

This time she didn't hesitate. The men she'd fought alongside were already fleeing, and William would be joining her. She nocked an arrow, taking aim at any Englishmen who might run toward them while William remained directly in front of her. Protecting her.

Several men came at them and paid with their lives, by way of one of her arrows or the razor edge of William's blade. Through it all, he stayed so close to her, she could sense his body heat, anticipating his movements before he made them.

They melted into the edge of the forest but remained tense for a fight. There were more places for them to hide, aye, but just as many for their enemy to do so as well. William crouched low and motioned for her to follow, indicating they should duck behind a wide tree to their left.

He put a finger to his lips. Kinsey nodded, holding her breath, straining to listen.

Footsteps shuffled through the damp underbrush.

Her heart thundered in her chest. Surely, whoever was coming could hear it, thumping louder than their steps as they came nearer.

William reached for her hand, wrapping his warm grip around her. It was a small comfort, but it calmed her, nonetheless.

A twig snapped on the other side of the tree, followed by another scuffle of feet before the steps departed. "Nothing there."

Kinsey wanted to fall backward and gasp with relief. Instead, she exhaled slowly and tried to rein her heartbeat back into a normal rhythm. William held up his free hand, indicating they should wait a moment longer.

His other hand remained on hers, protective.

She studied him as the forest around them settled into silence once more. His dark, intelligent eyes with more lashes than any man ought to have. The stark handsomeness of his face. The fullness of those lips and how perfect they'd felt against her own.

Everything in her was alight with the feeling of being alive. The air had never been more refreshing; the earthy scents of the forest were stronger, crisper. She'd never felt more powerful.

In that instant, she wanted William, needed him, more desperately than ever before.

She didn't fight the impulsivity and instead rode it like a wave, letting it carry her the few inches between them to kiss him, hot and hard, on his sensual mouth. It was quick, a pressing of lips, a brushing of tongues, and then it was done.

The slam of lust was immediate. She was not alone, for his dark eyes burned with desire as he stared at her. His jaw squared with determination then, and he tightened his grip on her hand, quietly pulling her onward.

## ❧ 16 ❧

William didn't look at Kinsey again until they found the predetermined location by the river. He couldn't. As it was, it had been too damn hard not to draw her against him and finish the kiss she'd started.

Her fingers were so petite in his, the connection between them crackling like lightning. He should have dropped his hold on her when they'd reached his men, but he held her a moment longer. Too long.

Reid's gaze fell on them, and a single brow lift was all the reaction William needed. He slowly released Kinsey's hand. Tingles of warm pleasure lingered on his skin, a reminder of the sweetness her closeness brought.

William looked around at the faces and breathed a sigh of relief to see so many. They had lost very few, thanks be to God.

Many had even managed to escape with their horses, including Reid.

"It eases my mind to see so many of ye here," William said to his men. "The king's army will go to Jedwood Forest to recover. Ye may join him there if ye like, but I would like to try taking Mabrick Castle again with a different strategy than before, utilizing what we know now." He caught Reid's eye with a nod. "We are only two days away if we share the horses and can acquire more. The English won't think to follow us, no' when they're chasing the lot who are fleeing to Jedwood."

"Where ye go, we follow," Duff said.

The men around him nodded in agreement.

William's chest swelled with an appreciation for his men. "Ye're a good lot. I'm proud of ye."

His da might be sparing with his praise, but William never wanted his men to question his pride in them.

Kinsey stood off to his right, where she'd remained after he'd released her hand. He longed to look toward her, to reassure himself she was there, that she was safe, alive.

When she'd fought with the sword, he had feared he might lose her before he could get to her. And then she'd saved him. He bit back a smile.

"We willna need to share horses," Alec said. "There were several tied up a ways from here. Only two guards."

William could have crowed with delight. With horses, they could travel faster, and could sell some off for coin when it was needed. Whatever had been left back at camp was lost to them. "Will five men be enough to take them?"

Alec grinned. "Ach, aye."

"Go on with ye then." William jerked his head in the direction Alec had indicated.

Alec and four others rode off.

Kinsey was still nearby, the familiarity of her feminine scent teasing at his awareness. His gaze drifted toward her and caught on Reid, reminding William what needed to be done. "Reid, go on to Jedwood and inform Laird MacLeod of our intentions."

Reid grunted in acknowledgment, and William's attention shifted back to his army. "When the men return with the horses, we ride."

They cheered their approval, and those with steeds prepared them for a ride that would be a couple of hours at least.

A quiet moment settled on William as the attention of others fixed elsewhere, without the need for action on his part. In that flash of a second, his stare found Kinsey's and met her bold, ice-blue eyes.

Lust pounded through his veins like fire, leaving him hot and hard beneath the padding of his gambeson. He let his gaze drift down her body, the fitted trews, the narrow leather belt, the white leine, now dirty and stained with a spot of blood.

He needed to bathe as much as he needed to sate his lust. An image rose in his mind, awash in a curtain of steam. A tub filled with hot, scented water and Kinsey. He wanted to plunge into that tub with her—slippery, wet skin and a frantic, eager joining.

Her breath quickened, evident by the rapid rise and fall of her bosom as if she too could see his thoughts. How he longed to cup her breasts in his palms and tease his tongue over those taut pink tips.

He swallowed and forced himself to turn away. "Duff," he called out in a thick voice. He cleared his throat as the man approached. "I'll need ye to ride ahead later to see if ye can secure an inn for our party or find a village with more than one inn, aye?"

Duff, of course, was quick to comply, and William filled the time waiting on Alec with planning where they might stop for the night. The conversation wasn't the distraction William wanted. Considering an inn for the night made William think of the bed he would be sleeping in, and the fantasy immediately following of who he wanted in that bed with him.

*Kinsey.*

His body ached for her. It had for the last several days. Every time his eyes met hers, or he caught the delicate scent of her, he was dragged back to that intimate night when his fingers had explored her so intimately. When they'd slept the night together.

Fortunately, it did not take long for Alec and the four others to return with several horses in tow, the animals still strapped with travel packs. "They dinna know what hit them, we came so fast." Alec tossed a leather bag high in the air and caught it. "Blighters had a good bit of coin on them too."

"Paying to lodge us in an inn, and providing a bit of ale and food, is the least the bastards could do." William leapt onto one of the horses.

He glanced back to ensure his men were ready and found Kinsey watching him, her cheeks flushed, her eyes bright in a way he recognized well enough to send heat rushing to his cock.

Lovely.

Strong.

Enticing.

Never had he wanted a woman so badly in all his life. And never had his heart been more at risk.

THE SUN HAD BEGUN TO SINK INTO THE HORIZON WHEN THEY finally stopped at an inn. Through the duration of the ride, Kinsey could not take her mind off William. How she wished that kiss could have lasted longer in the forest. Mayhap become more.

She'd hardly noticed the frigid wind several of the men groused over. Not when her body was burning up with longing, reliving the way his fingers had played over her sex, drawing out that incredible release.

It was a foolish thing even to waste time remembering when he'd resolved not to have her. He would be another woman's husband.

He could never be hers.

Why then did he keep watching her like he wanted to drag her into his arms? And why could she not stop herself from wanting him?

She needed a solid night of sleep, a chance to be alone with her torment. Behind a door that she could lock. She bided her time as they filled the inn, eating a hearty meal of freshly cooked venison and crusty bread. Through it all, William's stare continued to glide toward her.

She might have thought she imagined it, except that the serving wenches confirmed his distracted attention with their continued glares and spiteful resignation.

When enough time had passed that her departure would not bring attention, she pushed to her feet, bade good evening to the men and slowly climbed the stairs.

"I dinna ever thank ye." William's familiar voice came from behind her.

She didn't turn, not trusting herself to even look at him. "For what?"

He appeared at her side. "For saving my life." His voice was practically in her ear, low and intimate.

She repressed a shiver and kept her focus on the stairs. "Ye saved mine as well. Else I would have been fighting my blade and the Englishman all at once."

"Were ye injured?" He turned her gently toward him, and his deep brown eyes searched hers. "I dinna ask…"

She shook her head. "And ye? Were ye injured?"

He lifted a shoulder. "A few swipes with a hammer."

"I can look at them for ye if ye like." She made the offer without first thinking about how such an invite might sound when clearly, he would have to come into her room for her to do that.

Heat flooded her cheeks and she continued up the stairs. "That is—I mean, I could do it in the hall, or—"

Her thoughts jumbled together, and her heartbeat echoed through every sensitive place on her body. She continued on to the landing, wishing she hadn't made the offer.

"That's no' necessary." William followed her, not stopping until they reached her door. "Kinsey, I…"

Whatever made him hesitate was the very thing that made her press him to say what he'd intended. "Aye?"

"I dinna trust myself with ye." His gaze was locked on hers, each of them studying the other with an intensity that made it hard to breathe.

"Why?" she whispered.

His brows furrowed as if he were in pain. "Ye know why."

Her lips went dry. She flicked her tongue over them, and his attention drifted to her lips. "I do."

The muscles at his jaw flexed as if he were gritting his teeth. "I should go." He didn't move.

She nodded mutely but wished she could shake her head, to beg him instead to stay. As he'd done before.

He would have a wife someday, and that wouldn't be her.

William reached for her and gently caressed her cheek. Kinsey closed her eyes, reveling in his touch as an embarrassing little whimper rose from the back of her throat.

A moment passed, and his hand didn't move as she'd expected it to. As she'd hoped it wouldn't.

The spicy scent of him grew more apparent, and she recognized that he'd drawn nearer. His hand slipped to the back of her neck to cradle the weight of her head, and his mouth found hers.

His lips brushed hers. Sweet. Tender.

She could have cried at the beauty of it. At how greatly her soul had longed for this.

His tongue was gently prodding at her lips, which she parted for him, desperate for the stroke. He deepened their kiss and pressed their bodies more firmly together. Hardness nudged against her belly, a telltale sign of his arousal.

Whatever control had tethered Kinsey until then snapped. Her kisses turned hungry, desperate, as did his, their bodies arching against one another. He nudged her back to the door and slid one powerful leg between her legs. She rolled her hips against him, so his muscular thigh rubbed at her sex. Her desire blazed out of control.

She needed him like air.

Footsteps echoed off the wooden boards, heading straight for them.

They should separate. Sir William ought to go to his own room, and she should be in hers. Alone.

She couldn't feign being aloof around him when she had given herself to such passion. She had to stop. To back away.

But how could she when the very thought made her feel as though she might suffocate without him?

One more kiss.

She kissed him deeply, determined to make the most out of the last one.

He adjusted his position, dragging his body against hers. His arousal pushed at the sensitive spot between her legs.

She sucked in an excited breath.

The footsteps came closer. Too close.

Her hand groped behind her at the door handle. She found the metal latch and opened the door, sending them both spilling inside her room.

William kicked the door closed and stood, staring at her, his breath panting.

"I should go," he said raggedly.

It was then she realized with certainty that their attraction to one another was too great to ignore. A passion that could not be cast aside, only sated.

She shook her head.

He drew her toward him, and their mouths clashed in a frantic kiss. His hands found her bottom and arched toward her, so his hard cock ground at her sex. She cried out, hoarse with lust.

His mouth moved down her throat, kissing and sucking. "I need to stop," he rasped.

"Nay, please." She clung to him. "Don't stop."

He shifted a hand from her bottom, up to her breast, trying to cup it where it had been bound against her with a thick band of linen. "I want ye so damn bad."

She looked at up him. "Then have me."

He hesitated. "I have to wed—"

"I know." She tugged the buckle of her belt free and let it drop to the ground. "I don't care." She yanked her leine over her head and met his gaze with a challenge. "I'll have ye any way I can get ye."

His gaze caressed her body. "Ye're no' fighting fair."

"Depends on which side ye're on." She loosened the linen crushing her breasts to her body and let the cloth unfurl to the floor. The last piece slipped off her bosom, and he gave a low growl.

She reached for him and unhooked the fastenings on his gambeson.

"I want to protect ye," he said in a low voice. "I canna be the one to—"

"I've told ye before." She peeled his gambeson over his shoulders and let one of her hands glide down his torso to frame the column of his arousal with the palm of her hand.

He was hot and impossibly hard. Her sex twitched. "I don't need protecting."

He cursed and dragged her against him, his mouth capturing hers as he drew her legs around his waist. Though their clothing separated them from one another, she was still splayed open for him, his thickness laying against her.

He carried her to the bed and lowered them both to the mattress. His mouth teased down her throat, and his hand went to her breast. He found her nipple with first his thumb, then with his mouth and tongue.

Fire and bliss spiraled through her. Kinsey gripped the coverlet beneath her, writhing for more, desperate for release.

His hands moved over her trews as he loved her breasts.

There was a little tug at her ties, then her bottoms were pulled away, and cool air washed over her fevered skin. He caught one nipple gently between his teeth, while his fingers found the juncture between her thighs.

Her skin tingled with impossible sensitivity and sent heat surging to her core. She cried out and spread her legs.

She needed more, or she might explode.

He eased lower and looked up at her with a flicker of mischievousness in his dark eyes. He caught her thighs with his upturned palms and opened her legs wider to reveal her sex to him. Watching her, he leaned forward and slid his tongue over her center.

Pleasure. Immediate and instantaneous.

Her head fell back with its intensity, and he lapped at her again. His tongue was merciless as he indulged her. His finger eased inside her, probing while his tongue flicked and circled, teased and tasted.

Whatever wound tight within her could not coil any further and broke free with a force that left her crying out. William's mouth covered her, stroking her with his wicked tongue as she climaxed.

When she finally floated back down to reality, he eased off her and divested himself of his leine. Firelight rippled over his muscular torso and made her fingers ache to run them across his banded flesh.

Pink skin showed on the scar where she had sewn the arrow wound with her untrained hand, and shadows splotched his torso where he'd been struck in battle.

His hand went to the fastenings of his trews. "Are ye certain?"

Was she certain? She could have laughed at such a question were she not so hot. So...wet.

She could feel her need between her thighs, slippery and eager.

"Are *ye?*" She pushed upright to sitting and ran her hand lightly over his battered torso. His muscles were firm beneath the soft-ness of his skin and the sprinkling of coarse, dark hair.

He groaned, not with pain, but pleasure. "Only if ye are."

"I need ye," she said.

He tugged the ties of his trews free. His cock pushed out from the leather, jutting straight toward her. It was as thick as she'd expected, perhaps more so, and moved slightly with the beat of his pulse, which matched the one insistently thrumming at her sex.

Mayhap she ought to be nervous with a virgin's trepidation, but even after her release, or perhaps because of it, she wanted nothing more than the completeness of what was to come.

## ❧ 17 ❧

**W**illiam's mind was wild with lust. The battle earlier that day had left him restless, especially when coupled with the slow burn of wanting Kinsey for so long.

She regarded him from where she sat on the bed. Even as much as he longed for her, he couldn't help but stop and stare.

Her curls were tousled, her cheeks flushed, eyes sparkling with excitement, her focus drifting toward his cock. Her breasts were even more exquisite than he'd imagined, round and firm, tipped with small pink nipples. They were perfect. *She* was perfect.

More than perfect; she was his.

*His.*

In the haze of his desire, the word rang out in the purest note.

"Ye can touch me if ye like," he said hoarsely.

She glanced up at him, as though gauging his sincerity, then reached for him. Her slender fingers closed around his hard shaft, and a delicious thrill tingled through his body. He grunted at the potency of his enjoyment.

"Do ye like that?" She fluttered her lashes coquettishly up at him, employing the words he'd once used with her.

"Aye." He wrapped his hand around hers and guided her movements to slide up to the tip, then back down the shaft.

He removed his touch from hers, and she continued with the action, pumping her fist over his cock, her breasts jiggling slightly with the action. His ballocks drew tight.

He leaned his head back and closed his eyes. All his senses focused on the sweet stroke of her hand.

Air fanned over him. Before he could identify what had caused it, something warm and wet dragged across the swollen, sensitive head. His eyes flew open, and he looked down to discover Kinsey parting her lips to draw his prick into her mouth.

"Do ye like that too?" The heat of her breath caressed him.

He groaned and gave a stiff nod.

She licked him once more, this time on the underside. Her mouth brushed against the tip, circling it before suckling lightly.

He ground out a low curse. There would be time for showing her more of that in the future. For now, he had to have her, or he wouldn't be able to last much longer.

"I want ye," he said between gritted teeth.

She gave him another little suck at the head of his cock and hummed her response. The vibrations shivered down his shaft and reverberated through him.

*Jesu.* He was so close already.

"Ye'll no' have much more of me if ye keep up with that." He smoothed his hand over her cheek.

She slid her mouth off him, and he crawled over her, slowly urging her back onto the mattress. He skimmed his palms over her silky skin, pausing at her breasts where he drew first one nipple into his mouth, then moved on to the other. His tongue flicked over each nub in turn until it peaked into a hard tip. His cock pressed to her lower stomach, straining.

Kinsey angled her hips in an attempt to get beneath him. It would be so easy to thrust into her, to take her hard and fast until his release overtook him. But he knew she was a maiden.

In all the experience he'd had with women, he'd never deflowered a virgin. His hand balled into a fist in the bedsheets as he hesitated.

He shouldn't take her now.

Kinsey spread her legs beneath him and wriggled, so their pelvises were fitted together.

"Ye're a maiden," he said with ragged determination.

"Not after tonight." She squirmed, nudging the tip of him against her entrance.

She was hot and swollen, so wet that the head of his cock eased inside her.

Still, he held back. "I canna—"

"'Tis mine to do with as I choose." Her body moved with a sensual rhythm, encouraging him with every roll of her hips. "I want ye and have for a while. I made this choice."

His hips flexed against her, in time with the pace she'd set, his arousal slipping slightly deeper with every rock of their bodies against one another. Her entrance squeezed around him. So damn tight.

She leaned her head back and arched her breasts, moaning with enjoyment as she did so. One thrust. That would be all it would take.

Only he had to ensure she understood.

"I canna marry ye," he said.

Her lips curled upward in a coy smile. "I'm not asking."

"I dinna want ye to regret this if ye wed." He braced his body over her as she continued to coax him more deeply within her.

"Any man that weds me will know what he's getting."

It was true. Kinsey wasn't the type to allow herself to be married off. She would choose him, and he would know her thoroughly.

A spike of jealousy stabbed into William for whomever that man would be. For it would be her husband who would cradle her as she slept. The way William had done. The man she married would take her in bed night after night. He would know her and respect her. And she would love him.

William knew in an instant he wanted that man to be him. He wanted Kinsey for himself. Not just now, but later as well.

*Damn it.*

He caught her hand with his free one and braced himself with the other. He took her then, possessive and desperate, in one hard thrust. Her sheath was beyond tight, her grip almost painful.

But it was not his discomfort that concerned him. "Did I hurt ye?"

"Don't stop," she breathed.

He gritted his teeth against the squeeze of her core and moved carefully, slowly, as he drew out then back into her. Her brows tensed, but she continued to rock her body in time with his.

Slowly, her expression melted into one of enjoyment, and the grip around him loosened into one of pleasure. He quickened his pace, stroking into her until they were both panting.

The friction between them built with delicious sensitivity. He was close to his own release but refused to come until she did. He shifted his position, so he rubbed over the nub of her sex and pumped hard into her.

She wrapped her legs around him, drawing him deeper into her. The euphoric grip on him tightened as her cries pitched. Suddenly her core spasmed around his cock, enticing him toward his own orgasm. A low groan tore from his chest as it crashed over him, taking him to a place where stars flashed before his eyes.

Hot and cold all at once. Tingles dancing over his skin. And through it all, that incredible clench squeezing him as Kinsey experienced the same pleasure.

Finally, the world came back to him, starting first with Kinsey gazing up at him with a languid smile. Never had he seen anything more beautiful.

Never had he cared for a woman more.

The revelation was terrifying. They could never be, especially when he knew his obligation.

Even if she did possess his heart.

❧

LYING WITH WILLIAM HAD BEEN A MISTAKE. MAYHAP THE greatest, most exquisite one of Kinsey's whole life, but a mistake, nonetheless.

It was the first thought that came to her the following morning when sunlight framed the shutters, when the blaze of lust had long since cooled. He was behind her still, a wall of heat and strength, his arm protectively thrown around her.

It wasn't the act she regretted, for the pleasure she experienced was worth every brilliant moment. Nor was it the loss of her maidenhead, which had always been of little consequence to her. Nay, it was the effect the act had on her heart.

She'd meant for the intimacy to be something without meaning. The way men discussed it, the act was supposed to simply sate lust.

But as she lay in the cradle of his embrace, the intimacy between them made a place within her glow with unexpected warmth.

He shifted at her back and nuzzled her with his unshaven jaw, sprinkling kisses over her sensitive shoulder and neck. She shivered with pleasure.

"Did ye sleep well?" His voice was gravelly with sleep.

*Too well.*

Everything in her ached to arch back against him. "Aye."

His hand brushed down her naked shoulder. "Ye're no' too sore?"

She squeezed her thighs together, where there was a hint of

soreness, though it was nearly drowned out by the thrum of desire.

How could she want more of him when she'd been so thoroughly sated the night before? And if her heart were already falling into his palms, wouldn't it only hasten the path if she gave in to her need?

His hand slipped beneath the blanket and caressed her hip.

The pulse of desire quickened, and she found herself questioning if they would have time to couple once more, rather than mulling over reasons why she ought not to. "When must we depart?"

"Soon." He gave a low, sensual chuckle in her ear. "No' enough time to do everything I want." His hand left her hip and went to her face instead, turning her toward him. "Especially watching ye when ye climax."

Self-consciousness flooded her. Knowing he had observed her in such an uncontrolled moment scalded her cheeks with heat. "Why?"

"'Tis as though I can feel yer pleasure as ye experience it." He propped himself on his elbow and gazed down at her, taking his time, as if they had scores of it. "The way yer cheeks flush, how yer lips part around yer cries. That time ye came for me, I couldna clear it from my mind. I would harden at the mere thought of ye."

She recalled his solid arousal and a quiver of anticipation squeezed through her. *She* had done that.

"The men will be waiting for us." He brushed a kiss across her lips and pushed up from the bed. She'd enjoyed the front of his nakedness before. Now, she sat up to better follow his finely sculpted backside as he padded over the wooden floor to the ewer.

His broad back rippled with muscles at every small movement and tapered to a narrow waist and hips with a firm arse. A light sprinkling of dark hair covered his thighs and calves.

Aye, he was indeed a handsome, well-built man.

He tugged on his trews. "I'll return to my room and ready to leave from there."

His statement was a reminder of the ugly truth sitting between them: that their passion had to be kept a secret, and he would need to marry for his clan.

Not that Kinsey wanted marriage. It sounded like more rules and structure than she cared for, especially being a laird's wife, which was not a role she'd ever wanted. She craved freedom, adventure, the life she was living now. A man would only impede such liberties.

Or so she told herself.

William approached the bed with his gambeson untied, and his leine untucked and gave her a lopsided smile. "Dinna be late, my warrior." He lowered toward her and swept his mouth over hers.

With an affectionate wink, he snuck out into the hall and was gone. It wasn't until the door closed behind him and she was left alone that she longed for nothing more than to have him back at her side.

She roused herself from the bed they'd shared and washed as best she could. The Englishmen's packs they'd stolen had some clothing in them that had been passed between the men. There had even been one with trews and a tunic small enough to fit her. She dressed in the English clothes now, marveling at how costly they were. A squire's attire, no doubt.

William was already downstairs by the time she finished readying herself.

Duff slapped him on the shoulder as she approached. "I saw ye creeping back to yer room no' an hour ago. Where were ye at, pray tell?"

William smirked in response.

"Ach, then ye *were* with a lass." Duff nudged him. "He always gets closed up when he's spent the night with a wench."

Something gripped Kinsey's heart. Dread. Humiliation. Shame.

What would they all think of her to know she'd been with him? Would they presume she would receive different treatment?

"Was it the blonde with the..." Duff cupped his hands in front of his chest and waggled his brows. "Or the brunette with the wide arse?" His hands expanded to frame an imaginary bottom. "I personally had my eyes on that backside for the better part of the—"

Alec nudged him hard in the ribs. Duff shot him a dirty look before taking a second glance at Kinsey. His hands fell, and he gave her a sheepish smile. "Eh...did ye want some ale before we go?"

The men tried to refrain from talking about their sexual exploits in front of her. But now Duff's swiftness to cover it told her they didn't realize the woman William had been with was her.

Kinsey scoffed to cover up her surprise.

They didn't know. It was almost too good to be true.

William speared him with a glance. "Ye know better than to talk like that in front of a lass, Duff."

"'Tis nothing I've not heard before with this lot." Kinsey reached for a slice of bread and bit into it as casually as she could with her pulse racing like a warhorse.

The men laughed in reply, and Duff's cheeks grew red even as he joined in their laughter.

"Enough out of ye." William waved his hand at his army. "We'd best get to it before the rain starts."

The men left the inn with Kinsey following behind them. Only then did William's gaze catch hers. Aside from the brief moment they locked eyes, nothing on his face or stance suggested anything that had transpired between them.

The flip of her stomach, however, did.

Right along with the crash as she realized it might have been only the one time for him. Mayhap he wanted nothing more to do with her now that he'd had her. He hadn't mentioned seeing her again that night or any other night.

Despite the hard knot of dread, she knew if that were the case, it would be for the best.

For how else could she possibly guard her heart against the likes of Sir William?

## ❧ 18 ❧

William had never not known how to act around a woman before. Not until Kinsey.

After all, his previous trysts hadn't needed to be hidden. He was all too aware of how she felt about the others knowing of their intimacies. It had been plain on her face when she'd paled at Duff's claim that he'd been with a woman.

And he was all too aware of how the others would perceive her.

What was more, he'd never been in danger of caring too much. There had always been a mutual agreement: lust without love.

Following that logic with Kinsey was impossible. He could no more halt the way of his heart than he could cease his own need to breathe.

He kept his gaze averted from her, avoiding her for the duration of their journey to another inn on the Scottish side of the border. It would result in a longer ride to Mabrick for scouting, but it would ensure they could reach the castle for observation without being seen.

William would do everything right this time, starting with letting his men enjoy a night at the tavern before they began spying on the castle.

They were gathered downstairs when a tavern wench with a pouty smile winked as she passed him.

Duff nudged William. "Looks like ye already caught the attention of the bonniest lass here."

William stared hard at his ale to keep his gaze from wandering toward the true bonniest lass in all of Christendom.

"Keep on with that chatter, and ye'll end up with an arrow in yer arse from our bonny archer." Alec grinned down the table. "Eh, Kinsey?"

"My aim is better than that," she countered with a playful edge.

William looked toward her long enough to see a confident smirk on her lips. She tossed her head, tilting her chin away from him, playing as innocent to their affair as he did.

The serving wench approached their table with several mugs of ale. She passed them out, saving William's for the last, then he bent over as she set it in before him with a wink. "My, my." Her stare dragged down him with appreciation. "Ye're a fine one."

William was keenly aware of how close Kinsey was, what she would see and hear. But he also knew his men would question anything different in his reaction.

"Ye're a fine one yerself," he flattered.

"Ach, ye think so?" She straightened with her hands on her hips, glancing down at her ample bosom. Her gaze caught on a droplet of ale she'd spilled atop one round breast. She swept her finger over it, capturing the drop and sucking it from her finger, her eyes fixed on William.

"The sweetest ale in Scotland, I wager." He winked at her.

Her full lips curled into a slow, sensual smile. "Ye should taste it for yerself."

She was a bold one—the kind of woman he used to like.

Except now, her invitation made him cringe. The kind of man he'd been before made him cringe as well.

He must have taken a while to respond, for Duff spoke up beside him. "If he'll no' do it, I will."

Her gaze slid to Duff, and she winked before whisking off to another table.

"I figure ye werena interested." Duff shrugged. "I couldna let a hot invitation go cold."

William chuckled. "Help yerself."

Duff followed the woman across the room with his eyes. "I believe I'll do just that." He pushed up from the table so fast that he nearly spilled his still-full ale.

He wasn't the only one to get to his feet. Kinsey followed suit. "Forgive me. I'm rather tired this evening."

The men bade her good night as she left the table, her back stiff.

*Damn.*

William wanted to get up and follow her but worried it might make his actions look obvious.

And mayhap his being overly concerned about every one of his damn actions was making him act strangely. Damn it—he hated this.

He would do well to keep to his own room going forward. Matters of the heart would only complicate his duty.

Even still, after he finished his ale, he did not order another. Nay, instead, he found himself making his excuses and climbing the stairs. As he did so, it wasn't his room where he went, but to Kinsey's.

He rapped gently.

And received no reply.

"Kinsey," he called in a quiet voice.

Nothing.

He rapped again.

Still nothing.

He knocked yet again, and the door flew open. Kinsey grabbed him by the leine and dragged him into the room before slamming the door shut.

Her cheeks were scarlet, her eyes flashing a brilliant blue. She was vivid with life and rage.

Dear God, she was beautiful.

And he was hard as stone.

"Why can't ye just leave me be?" she demanded.

He stepped toward her. "Because I havena stopped thinking of ye."

"Ach, aye." She nodded with apparent disbelief. "'Tis why ye've barely looked at me all day, let alone spoken to me."

He frowned. "So the men wouldna suspect us. I thought ye dinna want them to know..."

"I don't." Hurt blazed in her eyes. "But ye didn't have to be so damn convincing."

The need to ease her pain consumed him. "I did it for ye." He reached for her, wishing to soothe her troubles. "What would ye have me do, Kinsey?"

She tilted her face toward his and met his eyes. "Why don't ye go downstairs for more of Scotland's sweetest ale?"

Ah, so that was it. She was jealous. That was an emotion he could handle.

"Who wants ale when there is whisky?" He cupped her face, determined that she see his longing for her. "Fiery. Intoxicating," he murmured. "Leaves ye craving more and more."

The ferocity in her eyes softened. "William." She said his name with resignation, with wanting.

A wanting that simmered keenly in his own blood.

He lowered his mouth to hers, uncertain if she would respond to his affection with a kiss or a bite. Regardless, it was worth the risk.

*She* was worth the risk.

Her lips parted for him, and her arms curled around the back of his neck. His hands glided down her body and pushed her against him. She gave a desperate whimper.

"I was trying to protect ye," he said between kisses.

She leaned away from him and regarded him with an anxious expression.

He dragged her back toward him and ran his mouth down the smooth warmth of her neck. "What is it, my Kinsey?"

Her head fell back, exposing the graceful column of her throat. Which would lead him down to where her bosom heaved up and down. But it was nothing he would force on her.

He hesitated and regarded her. "Do ye want me to leave?"

She stared at him, panting, her eyes wide, and for the span of a moment, he feared she might actually tell him to go.

Kinsey should tell William to leave.

She stared into his worried brown eyes, and her heart slipped deeper into him. Her head spun with giddiness, and her pulse hummed with a delicious heat throughout her body.

These were the sensations he aroused within her that she loved. The others, the bitterness of jealousy, the wounded uncertainty at his indifference, those were the ones she hated. Aye, they could tell the men of their affair and end the secrecy, but what would it matter when he would eventually wed another?

She held tight to him, their eyes and souls locked together. Pain and pleasure blended as one, a need to tell him to leave and a greater pull for him to stay. She couldn't allow this to continue.

This would have to be the last time.

Rather than reply, she drew him back toward her and kissed him. He groaned into her mouth as their passion exploded.

It was a wild, desperate coupling, both so eager for the other, they couldn't bother with removing all their clothing. William pushed her to the wall, pinning her there with his body as his hands worked at her trews, which were hastily shoved away as she undid his.

He had her there against the wall, with hard, frantic thrusts that had them both crying out. They reached climax at the same time and sagged against one another.

Kinsey's legs trembled with the force of her release, but her racing heart ached for what would need to come next.

"I can't do this again," she said quietly.

He regarded her with alarm. "I'll protect ye from the men. They willna find out."

She shook her head, tears forming in her eyes as the haze of lust burned away, leaving her with the stark reality of their circumstances. "The only protection I need is from ye."

His brows drew together in a pained look as if she'd physically wounded him. "Have I hurt ye?"

"Not yet." Emotion rose in her throat, unexpected and unwanted. "But ye will." Tears welled in her eyes, but she turned away so he couldn't see them. "I thought I could do this. That I was stronger..."

He lifted her face to look at him. "Kinsey..."

"If I keep on like this, I...I..." She couldn't force the words out, but they echoed within her, visceral pangs of agony.

He rested his forehead on hers. "I dinna want to hurt ye."

She dragged in a ragged breath and closed her eyes, unable to look at him as she made her final request. "Please leave."

He gave a hard exhale that recalled her attention to him as he drew away from her. Beneath his untucked leine, his fingers worked at his trews to secure them once more.

"I'm sorry," he said hoarsely.

She knew he was.

He stepped back from her, his handsome face lined with a disappointment that tempted her to change her mind. "I'm so damn sorry." Then he unlatched the door and was gone.

If she'd thought his departure would make her feel better, she was wrong. Her body glowed with the aftermath of their shared pleasure, his seed still within her. The scent of him lingered on her skin.

An ache settled deep in her chest and expanded until it was nearly choking her. Tears welled in her eyes, and she finally succumbed to the need to cry.

The night was long, followed by an overly bright morning that contradicted her foul mood. Too little sleep and too much thinking were an ill-matched pair if ever there were one.

If William was as deprived of rest, he didn't look it. He compiled a schedule to watch Mabrick Castle with his usual efficiency in an effort to keep track of the comings and goings at the front gate.

William was on the first watch and requested several of the men join him, along with Kinsey. It was not abnormal from what he usually requested of her. However, she'd hoped that in light of what had transpired between them, he would place her in another group.

She wanted to hate him.

It would be so much easier than the heaviness between them as they rode into England or the way her heart quickened when his leg rested near hers as they hid in the brush.

Regardless of her hurt, she couldn't hate him. Not when they had shared so much with one another: experiences, thoughts, intimacies.

Though she had never been in love, she knew of its razor edge. Her mother had been sliced by it with a wound that cut her to the quick. If Mum lived to be a hundred years, she would never get over the death of Kinsey's da.

With a painful example in such close proximity, Kinsey should have known better.

With that thought, she realized what she needed to do. It was time to go home. There would be no more raids where she would watch innocent people be slaughtered, and she would have no more blood on her hands. And her heart could be kept safe forever.

Aye, home—to Castleton—away from war and death and any hope of love.

## ❧ 19 ❧

O ver the next sennight, the days passed in a blur as the watch on Mabrick Castle revealed all the activity William needed to know for an attack. Each day around noon, there was a delivery of some sort, which meant there would be an opportunity to get into the castle.

While there were guards, the numbers weren't overwhelming, and based on their previous experience with the *pot-de-fer*, it could only shoot straight. If the army kept off the parapet, they would be safe from its wrath.

William was ready to announce to his men that they would be attacking the following day. A decision he was further convinced to be the right choice when he went downstairs in the morning to find Reid having a bit of bread and ale at one of the tables near the back.

Reid nodded in silent greeting toward William. "I was hoping this was the right inn. The others were too empty to accommodate so many."

William chuckled. "How many others did ye go to?"

"Only two." Reid took a sip of his ale.

The blonde tavern wench with the pouty smile approached the table. "And who is this?" Her gaze lit with interest as she scanned over Reid.

He ignored her suggestive tone.

Nonplussed, she turned her attention to William. "What can I get for ye?" She pursed her lips after she spoke, plumping them out in an obvious attempt to show off her most attractive feature.

Her flirtation reminded William of the first night they'd arrived, when Kinsey had been jealous of the woman. If she was still jealous, she didn't show it. Indeed, Kinsey scarcely spoke to him. At least outside of anything regarding her tasks as an archer.

For his part, William kept his distance from the tavern wench and any other woman who showed him interest.

It wasn't necessarily to please Kinsey. She'd apparently made her choice. One that his circumstance had forced on her.

Nay, his dismissal of women had everything to do with how hard it was to even think of another lass when his head and heart were too full of Kinsey. And how could he stop thinking of her when she was around him every day, vibrant with her determination to be the best damn archer Scotland had to offer?

William ordered an ale, and though the tavern wench gave him a pretty smile, she didn't bother with excessive flirting. She already knew of his disinterest.

After she departed, he regarded Reid. "Laird MacLeod?"

"I found him," Reid said. "He's hale and hearty as always. Lost a few men in the attack, but wasna injured himself."

While William was glad his father wasn't hurt, he didn't find the news surprising. His da always managed to come out of any situation unscathed.

The wench dropped off William's ale. He nodded his thanks and took a sip. "And his opinion on Mabrick Castle?"

Reid slid a chagrined look his way.

"He's no' pleased, I take it," William surmised.

Reid's mouth flattened in a hard line. "He thinks 'tis a waste of time. He would have preferred ye join the king and his army in Jedwood Forest."

Laird MacLeod's displeasure only increased William's resolve. His da would change his mind once Mabrick was taken.

"We will attack tomorrow afternoon," William said quietly.

"Then, I appear to have good timing." Reid lifted his ale in a silent toast.

That afternoon, William met discreetly with his army to inform them of his decision to take the castle the following day. Their excitement hummed in the air like the currents in the air just before a lightning storm. A week of monitoring Mabrick had not provided nearly enough activity for men who were used to constant movement of some kind.

William tried not to look at Kinsey as he spoke, despite his acute awareness of her bright blue gaze locked on him.

The men disbanded once he finished, going off to enjoy the rest of the day he'd given them to take for themselves. After all, for some, it might be their last afternoon of life. He never took for granted the dangers of battle.

It was rare to enter any fight without a single casualty, and there was nothing William hated more than losing a man.

Kinsey did not leave with the rest of his men and instead approached him.

His heart thundered in his chest. Reid apparently saw her coming and quickly slipped from William's side, leaving him more nervous than he'd been since he'd flirted with his first lass as an adolescent.

Impending battle always left apprehension pulling taut at warrior's nerves. Mayhap she sensed that and wanted companionship.

The idea of being with her again elicited a thrill of eagerness inside him. Not just the anticipation of intimacy, but to be in her presence once more, to revel in her tenacity and the passion she held for life.

Preparing for the battle was a welcome and much-needed distraction from the emotions otherwise roiling around inside William. All of which rushed back at him now in a dizzying maelstrom of elation, hurt and hope.

She stopped before him and met his gaze, her face absent of affection or any other telling expression.

Something cold locked around his heart.

"After we take Mabrick Castle, I'll be returning to Castleton," she said flatly.

*Castleton.*

He would never see her again.

The news was a crushing blow. Not only had he lost Kinsey, but he'd also lost their archer. He shielded his emotion behind a nod of understanding.

He'd ruined any chance with her, and now he'd ruined his army as well.

She took a quiet breath, as though preparing to say more, when she gave a curt nod and strode off. Tempting though it was to recount the scant conversation in his mind over and over and over again, he had the details of their attack to plan.

He spent the rest of the afternoon and evening with Reid, perfecting the final details. The next day, just after the sun indicated noon, William and his men hid in the forest on the path leading to the castle entrance with Kinsey in the brush, her bow ready.

As expected, the rattle of wagon wheels rolling over the hard-packed trail echoed through the trees. It came into view with covered bales of hay and only one driver.

William held up a single finger to Reid, who refocused his attention on his target and leapt from the foliage like a wild cat, swift and silent. He caught the man before the merchant could even cry out, squeezing at his neck with a powerful forearm.

Alec jumped onto the wagon, controlling it as the man struggled before finally slumping forward. Reid dragged the merchant's limp body from the carriage, where he was divested of his tunic, tied up and left in the forest to be found eventually. No more men needed to die than was necessary.

Reid appeared from the forest once more, wearing the man's tunic, and climbed onto the cart as several men slid beneath the heavy canvas covering the hay. William stepped forward to join them when a gloved hand folded around his. He looked back to find Kinsey at his side in full chain and armor, per his orders.

It was almost impossible to make out her expression beneath her helm. "Be safe," she whispered.

He gently ran his thumb over the back of her hand. Though he couldn't feel the action any more than she could in their gloves, his memory recalled the silkiness of her skin. "And ye, my love."

Her eyes widened, but he turned away.

The time had come to take Mabrick Castle.

And this time, he would not accept failure.

***

THE ANXIETY GRIPPING KINSEY HAD BEEN UNEXPECTED. THEY had been in battle before, but not like this. Not after having been so soundly defeated on their last attempt.

William had explained that it didn't appear the *pot-de-fer* had the ability to reach them from its position on the parapets. At the time, such information had put Kinsey at ease.

Her stare followed the wagon as it made its way toward the castle gates. Beneath the canvas were warriors who had become friends, as well as the man she loved.

There was no point in denying her feelings, even if she meant to run from them when this was all over.

The rest of the army that had not hidden in the wagon shifted closer toward the castle in preparation to storm inside the fortified walls once the portcullis opened. She nocked an arrow and waited for her chance to defend them.

It was almost impossible to keep her breathing even as the shout of an English guard calling down to Reid echoed in the damp air. Somehow, Reid managed to keep his accent neutral as he replied.

The guard's response did not come immediately, and the stretch of silence filled with tension. At least for Kinsey.

The late November chill had left her teeth chattering only hours before. But now sweat prickled at her brow.

What if the guards didn't believe Reid? What if they were suspicious and attacked the cart where William and the others lay defenseless beneath the canvas?

"Aye, come in then," a man shouted from the castle wall.

Kinsey gasped out the breath she'd been holding.

A loud creaking groan sounded, and the iron portcullis slowly began to inch upward. Where fear had once presided, now Kinsey felt a surge of hope.

*They'd done it.*

Her back burned from holding the arrow in place, but she didn't dare move. She would be their first line of defense until William and the men were inside.

Finally, the portcullis was raised enough for the wagon to pass under. Reid drove it into the bailey, stopping when he was almost completely through.

William and Duff jumped from the back with iron spears in hand. But they were not weapons. The spears were like double-ended tridents, with one end an open brace to catch the heavy gate, and the other flat with four thick arms branching out to hold it in place. These were lodged at the base of the portcullis as the other men leapt from the wagon and poured in from outside the castle walls.

The English did not hesitate to attack.

And Kinsey was ready.

She released her arrows, one after the other. Now, after having had experience in battle, she was better able to aim for debilitating injuries rather than kills. A kneecap, a hand, the arm they used to wield their weapon. It was far better than the throat.

A wall of Englishmen formed at the entryway to keep William and the army out, but after several minutes of combat, the Scots were able to force their way through. Their blades flashed and slashed, hacking through the defenses to get into the castle beyond.

Once they were inside, it would be easy to take possession of the castle, with most of the English's prime defending soldiers already slain.

Kinsey held back from sending more arrows into battle lest she hit one of her men. They pushed farther into the thick stone entryway and finally disappeared inside. Her heartbeat quickened.

This was it.

The hard part was done.

Victory would be theirs.

She searched the area for any guards who might be coming to assist. Seeing none, she waited.

That had been the plan. She was to remain on the outskirts of the castle, vigilant for any approaching guards. The seconds passed like hours.

It was impossible to gauge the time. The clashing of swords continued to ring out through the entryway, as did the grunts and cries. She craned her neck but couldn't see inside.

Apprehension tingled up her spine.

Shouldn't the fighting have stopped?

William had made it seem as though once they were within the castle, Mabrick would fall. The sounds of battle suggested otherwise.

She waited only a moment longer before making the decision

to relinquish up her post and join the men inside. Wasn't this why she had a sword strapped to her belt? In the event that she might need to help?

She scanned the surrounding area constantly as she moved, on alert for any men who might try to attack. Blood darkened the path where the packed earth met fitted stonework. She stepped over one dead English guard and another, flinching as she saw one of their own too—a man with unruly dark hair and a witty sense of humor.

She knelt at his side, but his open sightless eyes told her there was nothing that could be done. He was already dead.

The ringing of swords was louder now. She pressed against the thick stone wall and crept deeper into the entrance. There were more bodies, the floor wet with blood. The coppery scent mingled with the odor of death and made bile rise in her throat.

She lowered her bow and nocked an arrow to her side, still keeping it at the ready lest she need it and glanced around the corner.

The air sucked from her lungs in horror. Many of their men had been slain, but not only by English guards. Mabrick had reserved its most powerful warriors for inside the castle. Several Englishmen in superior armor, wearing blue and white surcoats, fought alongside the guards with brutal force.

In only one slash, the soldier closest to Kinsey blocked the blow of three men, killing one and injuring another as the third staggered back.

The back of her neck tingled with fear.

Her gaze darted through the mass of fighting men, seeking William. She found him alongside Reid as they battled against the tallest of all the superior English warriors.

William wouldn't want her to fight. She was aware of that, just as much as she realized that in joining this battle, it might result in her death.

But if she did not, William would certainly be slain.

Ignoring all the warning protests in her mind, she took aim and released her first arrow.

She had joined the fight.

## 20

This was not how the attack was supposed to go.

William ducked to evade the sword streaking toward him.

The skilled English fighters had been behind the back of the guards, waiting to defend the castle. This was a tactic he'd never seen before. Usually, the best fighters were at the head of the attack, not at its rear.

Reid rushed at their opponent and knocked him back several feet. After years of fighting together, William and Reid had formed a companionable rhythm in battle. One instinctually knowing when to attack while the other blocked.

Thus far, it had kept them alive.

Something flew across the room, snagging William's attention. The item had moved so fast, he hadn't had time to recognize it until the thing stuck fast in the arm of the man Duff was fighting.

William's blood turned to ice.

An arrow.

Kinsey was there.

"William," Reid hissed.

A mail-clad fist slammed into William's helmet. His head knocked hard to the side, throwing his balance off.

"She's here," he grunted.

Footsteps shuffled in front of William as Reid stood before him while he recovered. "She made her choice," Reid ground out.

A sharp clang of striking metal as Reid parried another blow pulled William back to the fight at hand. But even as he worked with Reid, jabbing and blocking, William couldn't take his mind off Kinsey.

He'd lost men. Their blood ran with that of their English enemies underfoot. He wouldn't now lose her as well.

With a guttural roar, he charged at the man with everything in him. No matter how powerful his opponent, fighting two men at once was no small feat.

True to his suspicion, the Englishman was beginning to tire, and William's strike had the man stumbling backward. Reid punched his sword upward, just beneath their opponent's helm. Blood spurted from the wound and spilled out in a river of red down the surcoat, staining the white with a brilliant crimson.

William and Reid both took a moment to catch their breath and lower their weapons to quell the fire in their limbs. In that flash of a second, they both assessed the situation around them.

After they'd broken through into the castle, there had been ten warriors within. It had seemed easy enough until the first one engaged with unholy power. When the remaining nine attacked, several of William's men had fallen.

Another arrow flew through the air and sank into the knee of the same Englishman struck in the arm previously. The man fell to his good knee but continued to lash out with his sword. The blade caught Duff in the shoulder.

Before William could run to him, a Scottish warrior rushed out to Duff's aid, too petite to be a man.

*Kinsey.*

William was moving forward now, his focus locked on her. His blade flew without mercy, blocking every hit aimed toward him, slashing in retaliation.

She stood up to the injured fighter who was nearly her size when he knelt. He pulled his blade back, but before his weapon could fall, Kinsey had whipped the bow off her back, nocked an arrow and sent it into his neck. He fell back and did not move.

Kinsey did, however. She caught Duff by the back of his chainmail and dragged him out of the fray.

She'd saved Duff. But how many were already dead?

He knew without a doubt, if they stayed, they would all be.

"Retreat," William shouted.

His men edged toward the entrance as they continued to fight. Kinsey, however, did not. Nay, she plucked arrows from her quiver and helped cover the men who were fleeing. In doing so, she'd taken the target from everyone's back and put it on her own.

One of the large guards turned on William and swung a massive two-handed sword. William dodged to the side, and Reid immediately struck their new opponent, slamming him in the chest with a powerful blow. In the time he did this, William had fully recovered and shoved the point of his blade into the man's helm while he reeled from Reid's hit.

By the time the English guard fell, nearly all of William's men had cleared out. He looked to Kinsey in time to see one of the elite warriors swipe his blade in her direction.

She drew her bow back, but the man was too close.

"Nay," William growled.

Another man jabbed his sword at William, obstructing his path to Kinsey. William opened his mouth to call for Reid to go to her but found that two men were already on his friend, their weapons flashing with lethal intent.

William kept his focus on Kinsey as she backed away from the man. A sharp blow caught William on the side of his shoulder. Pain radiated down his arm.

He needed to focus, to kill this bastard, so he could make his way to Kinsey.

Last time he'd had that thought, she had survived and come back to save him. He hoped to God her luck would hold out once more.

THE MAN WAS TOO CLOSE FOR KINSEY TO USE HER BOW. SHE dropped it and withdrew the sword she'd belted to her waist.

The Englishman struck out at her, his blade moving with such speed, she scarcely had time to dart from its path. She lifted her weapon. Her arms trembled with the weight of it, fatigued from her efforts with the bow.

Using its weight to accelerate her strike as William had shown her, she slammed her weapon at the man she fought. It missed him wildly. So much so, his helm turned to regard the blade's tip where it rasped against the stone floor.

His sword flicked up, too quick to stop. The hilt of her sword flew from her hand and clattered to the ground several feet away from her. Too far to retrieve.

Discreetly, she eased the dagger from her belt. If she were to die, she would take one or two of their enemy with her.

The Englishman advanced on her.

This time, it was she who was too fast. She skirted around him and struck hard at his side with the hilt of her dagger. He jerked in pained surprise, his tight grunt audible, despite the fight waging on around them.

He growled and swung around, not with his sword, but with his fist. It connected to her head, snapping it to the right. Her vision faded for a second, and the world around her tilted.

She staggered. Her body tried to keep moving, but her mind was stunned for that moment. A warning shrieked through her. She shook her head in the helm, trying to clear her thoughts.

Something powerful struck on her right side, exploding in pain and sending her sprawling. She hit the unyielding surface of the wall in another wave of agony and slid down.

A rhythmic whistle echoed in her helm. Wheezing. Her breath.

Fire burned in her lungs with each labored intake of air.

A shadow fell over her. All the hurt screaming through her faded beneath a spike of fear. If she remained where she was, she would be dead.

She squeezed her hand around her dagger and found nothing in her palm. She had lost it. Hopelessness nipped at her resolve. Brief, but sharp.

She gritted her teeth. It would be fists against steel, then. For if she were to die this day, it would be while fighting. She lifted her head to regard her opponent as he raised his sword.

Before he could swing it down, she launched herself from the ground and caught him at his waist. It had been her intention to drag him to the ground, but he was too solid, too powerful. He remained rooted where he stood and flung her off him.

Her head cracked back on the flagstones, and nausea churned in her stomach. Everything hurt. Moving. Breathing. Thinking.

The footsteps approaching her were heavy with intent. Even though her chest was on fire, the air pulling in and out of her chest came faster. Panic.

She tried to kick at the man, but her blows hardly touched him.

"Nay," William's voice rose above the din of war. "We yield," he cried. "We yield."

If they yielded, they would be hanged. It would be certain death for William and Reid.

"Nay." Kinsey shook her head. "Don't." Her voice was scarcely a whisper. Inaudible. He would never hear her.

Tears rushed to her eyes.

The Englishman standing over her grabbed her and hoisted

her upright. "I'll no' kill a man who is yielding." Though his voice was muffled by his helm, she caught the slight Scots accent.

The bastard was Scottish and fighting with the English?

She struggled against him, but he held his grip.

"Release her," William said fiercely.

She stopped struggling against her captor and searched the room through the slit in her visor, immediately finding William and Reid. Both had their hands locked behind their backs. They had surrendered.

For her.

"Her?" The man holding Kinsey turned her toward him, his grip loosening somewhat, becoming far gentler. "I wouldna ever have—"

He put his hand to the base of her helm and, before she could stop him, pulled it off. She glared up at him defiantly.

Let him see she was a woman. Let him see she had the grit to fight a man of his caliber. Let him see what a real Scot did for their country.

"Kinsey?" the man said in horror.

Confusion rattled about in her skull. Her head still ached from the times she had been knocked about.

Had the man said her name? She blinked in surprise. "What did ye say?"

"Kinsey." The man released her as if she had burned him and pulled off his own helm.

She stared in horror at the man she had been fighting, the man who had been seconds away from ending her life.

She swallowed around her dry throat, and when she said his name, it came out in a quiet exhale. "Drake."

*Where had they taken her?*

William paced the small cell in the dungeon. Reid sat in the corner with his head resting back against the wall. But William was too restless to join him on the filthy floor.

The last he'd seen of Kinsey was when the English warrior she'd been fighting ripped off her helm and stared at her. He'd then pulled his off as well, and she'd crumpled to the ground, unmoving.

Helplessness knotted in William's gut. He'd tried to free himself from the man holding him in place, to get to her, to safeguard her. The bastard's grip had been too tight on him.

Before William could ensure she was safe, the man without his helm hefted her into his arms and carried her away. What did they mean to do? Rape her?

Rage tore through him. If they so much as laid a hand on her, William would rip them limb from limb.

Footsteps sounded. He stopped abruptly and stared outside the cell to the narrow aisle dimly lit with a single torch. "Where have ye taken her?" he demanded. "What do ye mean to do with her, ye filthy bastards?"

His own voice echoed back to him. No reply followed. Though he hadn't been expecting one, emotion crumpled inside his chest.

"Mayhap they have a healer attending to her?" Reid said.

William cast his friend a hard look. "Aye, and afterward, they'll invite her to their victory feast."

Reid shrugged. "I dinna think they took her somewhere to kill her."

Mayhap she was already—

William slammed the lid on his thoughts, refusing even to let the words enter his mind.

"Did ye lay with her?" Reid asked abruptly.

William frowned at his friend's question. "'Tis no' any of yer—"

"They're going to hang us." Reid gave a mirthless half-smile of resignation.

It was true. They would be hanged for trying to usurp the castle. William suddenly understood Reid's point.

Footsteps echoed off the stone walls and thumped louder as the guard came closer. A tall man with dark hair stopped before the cell. The one who had taken Kinsey?

"Where is she?" William asked. "What have ye done with her?"

"She's no' any of yer concern," the man replied.

"A Scot?" William scoffed in disgust at the man's accent, at the side he'd chosen. "Ye do our people an injustice by siding with the English."

"Why did ye come here?" the traitor asked in an even tone. "Was it ye who attacked before?"

William glared at him. "This is my land, stolen from us when Balliol decided to yield Scotland's bounty to the fool English king." He curled his fingers around the cold bars of his cell. The odor of damp, dirty iron filled his nostrils. "I want it back."

"That willna happen." The man squared his shoulders. "Lord Carlyle is no' pleased about the number of men ye've killed in the two attacks. He is a good man and has agreed to hang ye rather than torture ye first, as other lords might have done in his position."

"How good of him," William said bitterly. "And what of Kinsey? The lass who was with us. Our archer."

"She's no' yer concern." The man's dark eyes narrowed, and a flash of a memory teased at William's thoughts. Before he could identify it, the recollection was gone.

His head ached from where it had been struck, addling his mind so his only focus remained on Kinsey's safety.

"She's every bit my concern." Panic scrambled in William's chest. He had to fight to keep it under control. Being irrational would not save her life. "She's with child."

It wasn't true as far as William knew, but it could be. They'd lain together twice. And mayhap it would spare her a few months in which she might somehow manage to escape.

Something flicked in the depths of the man's gaze. "What did ye say?" he bit out.

"She's with child," William repeated with more force. "My child."

The man's nostrils flared.

"What of Kinsey?" William demanded. "I can pay for her freedom. Tell yer baron that. Tell him to seek out—"

"Ye hang in the morn." The calm was gone from the man's voice, replaced with the chill of malice.

"Tell him to seek out Laird MacLeod," William finished.

But the man was already walking away, most likely not listening. Anger and helplessness exploded through William. "If ye touch her, I'll kill ye," William shouted into the darkness. He slapped an open palm on the bars in a strike that reverberated up the iron and echoed around them.

Kinsey should have stayed outside the castle. She was never meant to join the fight.

Regret soured in William's stomach. It was his fault.

He should never have taken her on. He'd been selfish, not realizing the risk he'd placed her in when he'd recruited her as his archer. All he'd thought about then was himself and what his army needed to win. To impress his father.

And now she would likely hang.

He sagged to the ground beside Reid.

This would be their last night alive, trapped in a cell with nothing to do but wait for death. After years of fighting together, now they would die together. And William wished it were any other way.

William's heart squeezed painfully.

Reid shouldn't have to pay the price with him. Nor should Kinsey.

She was too bright a light to be doused from this world. Her determination, too fierce. He would never hold her again, kiss her again, have the opportunity to tell her he loved her.

A stubborn ache settled in the back of his throat.

He should have told her he loved her. He should have told his father he would rather forego being laird, that he would marry no woman but Kinsey.

It was so easy to picture in his mind now, the idea of Kinsey as his wife. She was half English, aye, but she had the heart of a Scot. She was a warrior, powerful and beautiful.

He gritted his teeth against the hurt swelling in his chest.

He should have realized it sooner. Before it was too late.

Before now when everything was coming to an end.

"Do ye think they'll spare her?" William asked aloud the question burning a hole in his brain.

Reid looked down at the floor and pressed his lips together. "We'll find out on the morrow."

That was what William was afraid of. To go to his death with the pain that he had also killed Kinsey, the woman he'd been too afraid to admit loving.

He truly had lost everything.

❧

KINSEY'S BODY ACHED EVERYWHERE. EXHAUSTION FOGGED HER brain and left her thoughts thick as pottage.

Something pillowy cradled her body. A mattress? Was she on a bed?

How had she arrived there?

Flashes of memory came to her. Bodies. Blood. The sweep of a blade. Ducking away.

*William.*

Her heart beat harder, and her breath caught. A blaze of pain fired through her chest at her gasp. She groaned, a low, ugly sound that rose from her soul.

The last she'd seen of him, he'd been fighting. Had he made it? Had he been captured? Had she?

Somewhere nearby, a door closed.

Alarm spiked through her, and her eyes flew open. Anguish erupted in her brain at the light coming toward her. She put her hands to her face and moaned against the brilliance.

"Kinsey." The voice was soothing. Familiar.

The light shifted away, so the glowing red behind her eyelids faded to a soothing black. A quiet thunk came from the table beside the bed, and she knew the candle had been set aside. The splintering creak of old wood indicated someone sat on a chair near her bed.

"Kinsey, look at me."

She pried one eye open by sheer will and choked out a sob. Fire blazed in her chest. "Drake? Where is William? And Reid?"

Her brother, always so confident and sure, now looked at her with tears shimmering in his eyes. "Kinsey. I'm sorry. God forgive me. I dinna know—" He swallowed thickly and put his head in his hands. "I dinna know it was ye."

"Am I a prisoner?" she asked in a weak voice.

"I'm sorry, Kinsey," Drake repeated. "I dinna know."

She reached for him and gently pulled his hands from his face. "It wasn't yer fault. I didn't think ye'd be here, or I'd never have agreed to be part of the attack."

Drake scrubbed a hand over his hair. "The king has been knighting men for providing additional protection on the border. Lord Werrick knew how much I wanted it." His gaze wandered over her face, and issued forth a pained sigh. "I've no' been knighted yet on account of our Scottish blood, but if I do well here with Lord Carlyle..."

"They're going to make ye a knight?" Kinsey's heart splintered open.

*They were.*

Surely, they wouldn't award it to him now. The weight of her guilt hurt more than any of her wounds. He'd finally had a chance for the knighthood he'd worked his entire life to achieve. And she had ruined it for him.

Drake's lower lip trembled. "I've injured ye so badly." A tear escaped his eye. "I dinna know it was ye, Kinsey. God, I'm so sorry."

"Good thing I'm not so easy to kill, eh?" She offered him a smile.

He gave a shallow laugh. "Ye're a commendable fighter, little sister."

"I learned from the best." She grabbed his hand and held it.

He glanced down at their clasped hands, and his expression turned serious. "Do ye think...do ye think ye've lost the babe?"

Kinsey blinked at him, certain she'd heard wrong. "Babe?"

"I was told ye were with child." His face twitched in myriad emotions: sorrow, horror. Rage.

She shook her head and immediately regretted it as the room began to spin. "Nay. I'm no' with child."

"The man in the dungeon said ye were."

Kinsey stiffened. "William. He's alive? Reid too?"

Drake scowled. "Did he touch ye?"

"Drake," she cried out impatiently. Her chest was almost too tight to breathe, compounded by the press of fear. "Are they alive?"

"Aye, they're alive." Drake frowned. "But if he took advantage of ye—"

"I'm a grown woman," she said in a firm voice. "This is one of the reasons I left. Ye all think of me as a child. I'm a woman. I have fought in battles. I have made my own choices. And, aye," her throat clenched. "I have loved a man."

"And ye love him still?" Drake's brown eyes were hard, his jaw tight.

Exhaustion lapped at her awareness, promising her relief from her injuries. She closed her heavy eyelids. "I do."

"We've all been worried about ye, Kinsey," he said tenderly. "I should have insisted ye return home when I saw ye at the tavern. I hadna received the news ye'd left home so abruptly then. Ye should be at the manor. Safe. Ye shouldna have been here. I shouldna have—" His face stretched in a silent wince, and he rose abruptly to his feet.

Panic swelled in her. She had too many questions unanswered. "Where are ye going?"

"To find a way to get ye out of here," he said with stoic resolve.

"Ye can't." She reached for him again. "Don't sacrifice yer chance at knighthood for me."

Tears burned in his dark gaze. "I almost killed ye."

"But ye didn't." She shook her head. "And I can't leave. Not without William and Reid." The hurt exhaled from her wounded chest.

Drake turned from her.

She reached for him. "Wait, please."

"I have an idea." He said it so low, and her head swam with such discomfort, she wondered if she'd heard him correctly.

But before he could elaborate or confirm what she'd heard, he slipped out the door and was gone.

Kinsey turned her face toward the pillow and gave way to the wave of emotion drowning her. Because no matter the outcome, the cost would be far too great.

The night dragged on. The damp ground soaked through William's trews, and a heavy gruel with a rancid odor had been delivered unceremoniously to their cell, which neither William nor Reid had bothered tasting.

Not that any of it mattered.

Thoughts of Kinsey settled on his chest like a stone with such weight that it hurt to breathe.

A door banged in the distance and echoed through the dungeon, followed by footsteps. William leapt to his feet and cast a glance at Reid, who remained stony-faced as he stood.

It was impossible to determine in their windowless dungeon if it was already morn. Had the sun already begun to rise?

If so, then it was time.

Mayhap whoever came for him could give him news about Kinsey. Mayhap she might be able to live.

Such hopes were dashed when the familiar tall, dark-haired Scotsman appeared in front of the iron bars. The man looked left and right as if confirming no one else was nearby.

William's stomach dropped. It was the kind of thing soldiers did when they wanted to take care of prisoners on their own, with no witnesses. William remained toward the back of the cell. If the man were going to kill him, William would not make it easy.

The traitor stopped at the bars, looked in and beckoned William closer. William folded his arms over his chest and didn't move.

"Do ye want to know about Kinsey?" The man asked in an impatient whisper.

*Damn it.*

If William were going to be taken down by this bastard, at least it would be in the pursuit of doing everything he could for the woman he loved. William pushed off the wall and approached the bars. Though they were both unarmed, Reid took his customary place at William's right, ready to fight.

"What of her?" William asked, his voice quiet.

"She's hurt." Something flashed in the man's eyes, and his jaw clenched. "Verra badly."

The breath heaved from William's lungs in a wounded rasp, wishing her pain were his own to bear instead. "Ye did that to her," William said bitterly.

Was it just his imagination, or did the man flinch?

"Do ye love her?" The Scotsman asked.

Anguish screamed inside William's chest. "Do ye seek to use that love against me?"

"Do ye love her?"

"Aye." William held a hand over his heart. "I love her." The declaration echoed off the dungeon walls, reverberating all around them, resounding the truth of his words over and over again.

Those dark eyes narrowed. "She's on the third floor of the castle, first door on the left from the stairwell."

The information was so unexpected, William took a cautious step back. "Why would ye share that with me?"

The man put his hand slowly through the bars and unfurled his fingers. A thick metal key sat in the palm of his hand.

"What are ye on about?" Reid asked in a rumbling growl.

The traitor stretched his arm, extending the key to them. "This is the key to her room. Save her."

Reid looked to William, uncertain of what to do.

William hesitated.

Enemies didn't free the men they'd captured. They certainly didn't offer them keys with which to escape.

This was a trick. It had to be.

And yet if it wasn't...

William snatched the key. He curled it in his fist until it jabbed into his palm, proof that it existed. Assuming it was the correct key.

"Will ye save her?" The man asked, impatience edging into his otherwise calm voice.

This time, William did not hesitate. "Aye."

The traitor pulled a ring of keys from his belt and unlocked their cell. The door groaned as it swung open on its aging hinges.

William's body fired with a rush of energy, the same as before charging into battle. Even if this were a trap, it would be a chance to find Kinsey somehow, to save her.

Or, if nothing else, to say goodbye.

The man extended a dagger to William first—the ruby studded one his father had given him all those years ago—then Reid's dagger to him.

"We could kill ye," Reid said, accepting the weapon.

The man lifted a shoulder, his expression bland with indifference. "Ye could."

"Who are ye?" William asked. "Why no' see to her yerself?"

"Ye're wasting time." Without another word, the man walked away, putting his back to them.

It would be effortless to attack him from behind. But it would be without purpose when he had aided them in their escape.

Why had he helped them?

Reid cast William a skeptical look, clearly also uneasy with the scenario. They crept down the long hallway together and paused at the door. On the other side, there might be an army waiting to attack them.

But why would the Scotsman set up a ruse for them to think they were free and attack them, when they would just simply hang the next day?

William pushed the door, every nerve in his body on high alert. Nobody waited outside.

They followed the man's direction, climbing up three flights of stairs and stopping at the first door on the left.

"Fire," someone shouted from outside.

A distraction. Now William knew why the man hadn't seen to Kinsey himself.

There wouldn't be much time. He unlocked the door and entered the room. A still figure lay on the bed, with her bright red curls streaming over the linens.

*Kinsey*.

His heart caught in his chest, and he rushed to her side. He hadn't thought ever to see her again. "Kinsey."

Her eyes blinked open, squinting as though in pain, then widened. "William."

"We're escaping, my love." He pulled at her shoulder to help her up.

Someone had put her in a kirtle, one of simple blue linen that was rough against his fingertips. Kinsey winced as she struggled to sit, her breath labored.

A tight band squeezed at William's chest at the realization of her pain. She was tough, aye, but there was something delicate and precious about her that made him want to keep her protected. If given a choice, he would gladly assume her agony.

Once upright, she swayed, and her lashes fluttered as though she was near fainting.

She would need help to walk.

William looped one of her arms around his shoulders. "Reid, get her other side."

Reid rushed to comply, his actions swift but gentle. Even still, Kinsey flinched.

More shouts rose from outside as a fire was apparently being addressed.

William had wanted to ask Kinsey who the man was who had freed them from the dungeon, but now was not the time. Not when they had to rush. Not when they had to stay quiet and avoid being seen.

Together, Reid and William helped Kinsey down two flights of stairs to the main entrance of the castle where the stone floors were still tinged red from the blood of the battle. The cries of alarm came from somewhere in the rear of the castle.

They would be free to escape without notice.

"Stop," a voice bellowed.

William and Reid both began to run. Kinsey's body had gone limp between them. Surely, the pain had been great enough to make her lose awareness. At least that much was a blessing. William would not allow himself to think of any other option that would cause her to go so still.

An arrow skittered over the stone.

"Close the portcullis," another voice cried.

William increased his pace along with Reid, charging toward the portcullis as it began to fall closed. They had to make it. If they didn't, they would all be hanged.

Mayhap tortured.

A death cry came from the side of the portcullis where an English guard manned the lever. He slid to the floor, unmoving as the portcullis caught and held halfway down its track. The man who had freed William and Reid from the dungeon stepped from the shadows, his blade dripping with blood.

"Go," he shouted.

All at once, more guards appeared. The man didn't seem to notice as he charged into the Englishmen with his sword raised.

"There's too many." Reid eased Kinsey from his shoulders. "Go."

William hesitated in horror at what his friend was suggesting, even as he gathered Kinsey in his arms to keep her from sliding to the ground. "Nay."

"Damn it, William, save her." Reid snatched up a sword from the soldier who had fallen by the portcullis lever.

"Meet me at the inn," William said.

Reid gave a solemn nod, as if he were accepting an order that he would be able to follow.

They both knew the truth. There were too many English guards and only two men to stop them.

A band of tension squeezed at William's throat. Leaving his lifelong friend, his comrade in arms, went against everything inside his very soul. But he knew if he didn't go, Kinsey would die.

And Reid's sacrifice would be in vain.

William couldn't still his mind as he ran with Kinsey in his arms, fueled by the energy roaring through his veins. Reid, the boyhood friend, who'd been a part of his life for as far back as he could remember, would be dead. Slain by the English, as his family had been.

Kinsey was limp as William carried her and remained so a while later when he had to stop to rest his arms and back. He bent over her, panting for breath from his exertions, and found she'd gone pale.

"Kinsey?" he whispered.

She didn't move. Not so much as the flicker of an eyelash.

"Kinsey?" he said, louder this time, his voice hoarse.

When she did not respond again, he rested a light touch on her chest, confirmed it still rose and fell. However, the action was shallow and did not allay his fear.

She was still alive, aye, but for how long?

Tears filled his eyes, and he didn't bother to swipe them away. "Kinsey, stay alive, aye?" He cradled her to him despite his tired limbs and buried his face in the silkiness of her hair, breathing in the familiar sweet scent of her, though it made his heart ache.

"I love ye," he said vehemently. "I dinna want a wife from another clan. I want ye." He lifted her with arms that trembled with exhaustion and pressed onward on foot, desperate to get her to a healer. To see if she might be saved.

He would not give up. Never. He would do anything to ensure she lived.

EVERYTHING HURT.

Kinsey drew in a shallow breath and caught the scent of herbs in the humid air. Her back ached where she lay on a flat surface. She tried to shift her weight and pain sizzled in her lungs.

A noise caught in her throat.

"Kinsey?" an unfamiliar feminine voice asked. A cool hand settled on Kinsey's arm.

She blinked her eyes into a squint and found bundles of herbs hanging from the rafters, moving slightly on an unseen breeze. Her focus slid toward the shadow hovering over her and she opened her eyes so she could see properly. A woman was there, several years older than herself, with hair the color of honey and violet-blue eyes.

The woman smiled kindly. "I'm Fennela." She kept her voice low and soothing.

Kinsey frowned in confusion.

"I'm a healer," Fennela continued. "Ye've been injured. We're in my cottage, where I'm taking care of ye."

Kinsey's brow furrowed. She didn't remember coming to a cottage. Or being injured for that matter. Except that it hurt when she breathed, when she moved.

She searched her thoughts for the last memory she had and recalled Drake talking to her in Mabrick Castle. "William?"

Kinsey tried to sit up, but Fennela put a gentle hand on her shoulder to still her.

"He's resting." Fennela indicated the corner near the hearth.

William sat in a wooden chair, his arms folded over his chest, and his head tilted to the side. His face was relaxed with slumber.

"He carried ye all the way into Scotland from Mabrick Castle." She regarded him with admiration. "I canna imagine how difficult that must have been, even with ye being as slight as ye are. He must really love ye."

A flutter began in Kinsey's chest. It went cold and still almost as soon as it had started.

*Love.*

He didn't love her. And even if he did, he was meant to marry someone else.

The flash of jealous hurt passed almost as soon as it sank its teeth into her.

*He was alive.*

He was free of the dungeon and wouldn't be hanged. Even if he couldn't love her, she loved him enough to rejoice that he was safe.

Kinsey tried to rise, but the discomfort was too great.

With careful hands, Fennela aided her into a sitting position and propped her back against the wall. The pressure eased from her chest and allowed her to breathe somewhat easier.

"Is that better?" Fennela asked.

Kinsey nodded. "What's happened to me? It feels as though I'm breathing in fire."

"Ye've broken several ribs from what I can tell," Fennela replied. "Yer sides and back are bruised, and ye've taken quite the knock to the head. I suspect that is why ye were no' awake when Sir William brought ye here."

"Kinsey?" William leapt up from the chair and scrambled to her side.

Fennela gave a knowing smile and gracefully backed away.

William knelt in front of Kinsey and took her hand in his, which was still warm from his slumber. "Kinsey, thanks be to God, ye're awake."

"I heard ye carried me all the way to Scotland."

"I would do it again if need be." He reached toward her face and stroked her cheek.

It was a tender caress. A lover's touch.

Her pulse raced.

"William," she whispered.

The door clicked as Fennela left her cottage, giving them privacy to speak alone.

William gazed down at Kinsey. "I love ye."

Her chest ached, and she realized she was breathing too fast. "Ye can't. Please don't say such words to me when ye intend to marry another."

He shook his head. "Even if it costs me the opportunity to assume lairdship of Dunscaith, I willna marry another woman. No' when there's already one in my heart."

The world seemed to suspend at that moment. Her heart paused mid-beat; the air in her lungs froze mid-breath. All that existed was the warm clasp of his hand on hers and the way his brown eyes searched her face.

"Kinsey, I love ye," he said with a sincerity that resonated in her soul. "I canna promise ye a castle or wealth. I dinna know what I can promise ye, beyond a life with me and my eternal devotion."

"I don't care," Kinsey whispered. "I don't need a castle or wealth."

"'Tis well and good as we may no' have any of it." He gave her a charming grin that made her pulse run faster. "Knowing all that, will ye still marry me?"

Tears welled in her eyes, and she nodded, worried she might not be able to speak around the welling of happy tears in her throat. "Aye," she whispered.

William beamed at her. Not a tailored smile meant to be irresistible, but a genuine smile that crinkled the skin at the sides of his nose and corners of his lips and made his eyes twinkle.

A smile just for her.

He rose off his knee and curled his hand around the back of her neck, touching her as if she were a fragile thing that would break at first contact. His lips brushed hers, delicate as a butterfly's wing.

"I love ye," Kinsey said softly.

"And I ye." William nuzzled his nose against hers and slowly eased away. "I was a fool to try to abide by my father's wishes. It took me almost losing ye to realize I could never give ye up. No' for anything in this world."

"Don't think anything more of it." Kinsey embraced him as tightly as she could. "All that matters is that we're safe. That ye and Reid are not in the dungeon, or worse..." She shuddered, unwilling to even think of the alternative.

He looked away, but not before she caught sight of the flash of emotion on his face. Sorrow.

Ice threaded through her veins. "William," she asked tentatively.

His brow furrowed.

"How did we get out of Mabrick Castle?" She asked. "where is Reid?"

He drew a hard breath.

"William."

He looked back at her. "The Scotsman gave us a key."

Her stomach sank, and the pain in her ribs was so great, she could scarcely think. "The Scotsman?"

William nodded. "Aye, the tall one with the dark hair."

"My brother," Kinsey confirmed. "Drake."

William stilled. "Yer...brother?"

"Aye, the man ye saw at the tavern before our first attack on the castle."

William ran his hand through his hair, his face hard.

Alarm tingled at the back of Kinsey's neck. "What is it?"

"He set us free and gave us the key to yer room, along with directions to find ye, while he distracted the English."

"Nay." Kinsey's breath escaped her. This time, she welcomed the pain as penance for what she had cost Drake. "King Edward was considering knighting him." She shook her head and balled her fists in the bedsheets. "If he helped us, then he has so thoroughly betrayed them that he will never be considered for a knighthood." The pain in her heart was unbearable.

*What had she done?*

*What had she cost Drake?*

"That isna all he did." William pressed his lips together and a sadness so visceral passed over his features that Kinsey's body went cold with fear.

"What is it?" She asked. "What's happened?" Her voice trembled. "Reid?"

"We were attacked as we were leaving," William said. "Yer brother fought the English guards so we could escape."

Kinsey put her hand to her mouth. "Nay." There would be no saving him. If he were caught..."Where is my brother?" she demanded.

"He and Reid stayed behind to fight." William reached for her. "'Twas the only way ye would have survived. Ye were so injured, ye couldna even walk."

Kinsey pulled away from him, unwilling to hear anymore. "Nay," she whispered.

"Forgive me."

"'Tis not ye who needs forgiving." A sob caught in her throat and sent a streak of white-hot pain through her chest, a vicious combination of injury and emotion. "I'm the one who was too injured to move. If I could have made myself walk. If I could have—"

"They may be alive still..." William said, the hesitation in his tone indicative of his own lack of confidence.

Kinsey said nothing in response. What was there to say?

Drake, who had worked his whole life to ensure his family remained safe and fed, had finally sacrificed not only his dream but his very life.

For her.

To keep her safe.

Hot tears streaked down her cheeks. The price was unfathomable. She wished he would have left her to face the punishment she deserved.

And Reid...

William put his arms around her as she sobbed in shallow, painful gasps. They had their love, aye, but they had lost far, far too much.

## ❧ 23 ❧

Kinsey slept through the night, but only due to a tea Fennela had insisted she drink. Grief, however, was a heavy companion. One that tried to fight the drowsy effects of the tea, but was there, lodged in her chest like a stone, when she woke.

William was at her side immediately, his hand folding around hers with determined support. "We need to return to the inn," he said gently. "I need to speak to the men."

About Reid. To see how many were still alive.

He didn't need to say any of it aloud. Kinsey knew exactly what he meant. She nodded.

Fennela approached them with a small bundle of items in a swath of linen. "I have prepared a couple of teas for ye. One is to help ye with the pain and stave off infection. The other is to help ye sleep."

William looked up at her, shamefaced. "We havena any coin with us, but we do at the inn, I can bring—"

"The nearest inn is quite far away." Fennela frowned.

"Take this to guarantee my word that I'll return with the funds for ye." He offered her his dagger, the one studded with rubies.

"My da gave me this a long time ago when things were right between us." He gave a sad smile. "The value is more than we owe ye, but what it means to me is worth far more. I can assure ye I'll be back for it."

It was the same dagger Kinsey had once asked for in the wager they'd made so long ago. One he would have lost if he'd intentionally let her win. She hadn't realized what that meant to him until now.

Fennela put up her hand to refuse his offer. "Nay, I mean, 'tis too far to walk."

Heat washed over Kinsey. She was the reason they couldn't travel so far on foot. Helplessness had never suited her, and especially in a time of such sorrow and agony.

She sat up straighter and ignored the staggering pain squeezing at her lungs. "I can make it."

"Take my horse," Fennela said. "Ye may return it when ye bring the coin."

"Ye've put a lot of faith in us." William lowered his head humbly.

"'Tis a risk I'm willing to take to know Kinsey will be safe." Fennela rested a gentle hand on Kinsey's shoulder.

William regarded the healer with reverence. "I dinna know how to thank ye—"

She shook her head. "There's no need. Get to the inn and see that Kinsey has proper rest."

William looked at Kinsey, his gaze warm with affection. "Ye have my word."

They left shortly thereafter. William walked while Kinsey rode the small horse. They didn't speak much on the journey to the inn, both lost in their own thoughts, their own memories, as they grieved.

The sun was high in the sky when they finally arrived at the inn. Their arrival, however, brought on a new level of despondency. Getting to the inn had been a goal, something to move them onward. But now that they'd attained the small feat, what else was there?

William hesitated at the door of the inn, his jaw tight. Telling his men of Reid's loss would not be easy. Kinsey reached for his hand and held it firmly.

"I'll organize a party to go back tonight," William said. "To see if they'll allow us to..." he swallowed, "to collect those left behind."

The pain in Kinsey's chest had little to do with her damaged ribs as tears welled in her eyes.

Finally, William opened the door to reveal the army he commanded sitting around at the tables of the tavern. They turned at once.

Kinsey froze, staring in disbelief at the two men she'd thought never to see again.

Reid sat in the center of the group with a blackened eye and a cut lip. And at his side...

At his side...

Her knees went weak, and she sagged against William in a mix of overwhelming emotions, an eagerness to believe what she saw, but skepticism that it was some effect of the healer's teas.

Surely, it was too good to be true.

"Drake," she whispered.

He leapt up from the bench and came to her. His arm was bound in a sling, and he moved with a limp. "Kinsey."

His eyes filled with tears, and he gingerly pulled her toward him with his good arm. She fell against her brother's solid frame and clung to him.

"How?" She asked in amazed relief. "How did ye escape?"

"Yer brother is one of the fiercest fighters I've ever seen." Reid joined them. "I mean no offense." He nodded at William, who raised his hands in a show of surrender.

"Ye'll no' hear me argue with ye," he said.

"We pushed them back as we fought," Reid continued. "Drake

MADELINE MARTIN

told me to clear the portcullis, so I went behind it. He ran toward me and sliced through the rope in one blow. The portcullis fell as he rolled under it. The spikes slammed down and missed him by a hairbreadth. I've no' ever seen anything like it."

Drake shifted uncomfortably. He'd never been one for relishing praise.

"Ye could have been killed," Kinsey whispered.

Drake ruffled her hair in an affectionate gesture she'd thought never to experience again.

"Once we were outside, they couldna lift the portcullis without the rope, and we were able to flee." Reid patted Drake on the back and gave him a firm nod. "We found this bag of bones bleeding just outside."

Reid nudged Duff, who inclined his head respectfully toward Kinsey.

Her throat clogged, grateful to see him alive. To see all of them alive. She shook her head. "Drake, ye sacrificed yer chance to be a knight."

"I'd do it for ye all over again if need be." He gave her a tender smile and shifted his attention to William, extending his hand. "I'd like to clasp arms with the man who saved my youngest sister. Thank ye for yer bravery. And for trusting me."

"We couldna have done it without ye." William locked his hand around Drake's.

"If ye need anything, I'm yer man."

Kinsey's chest warmed at her brother's declaration of loyalty, knowing more than most how deep it ran.

"There is one thing I'd like to ask of ye..." William glanced at Kinsey with a grin.

Drake looked between them and narrowed his eyes. "Aye?"

"I'd like permission to wed yer sister."

Drake regarded Kinsey, who couldn't help but smile in reply.

He chuckled. "It seems she is in agreement." He nodded. "I can think of no one who would care for her better." His face tightened, and his voice lowered. "And after what ye told me in the dungeon, I confess I'm pleased to hear this request."

"Drake," Kinsey whispered fiercely.

He shrugged in response.

"William." A man's voice spoke abruptly from somewhere behind Drake.

They turned to see Laird MacLeod standing several paces away, staring at William, his expression hard. Kinsey's stomach tightened. She wished she could say something, to stand up in defense of William and the defeat at Mabrick.

But it wasn't her battle to fight, as was evidenced in William's determined wide-legged stance and the note of resolve in his eyes.

❦

WILLIAM KNEW WHAT WAS COMING AS HE LOOKED INTO HIS father's stern face. Disappointment.

He strode toward Laird MacLeod, bracing for the slice of his words, reminding William of his many failures. This time, however, William would not let them cut.

Nor would he allow his father to lay the path for his future or declare Kinsey unfit. Nay, William would forgo the lairdship and continue life as a soldier for the king. And he would wed Kinsey.

Never again would William put himself in a position where he might lose her.

"William," his father said again.

There was a tightness to his father's voice. Unfamiliar.

If William were not so set in his determination, it might have given him pause. He stopped before Laird MacLeod, feet braced, determined to fight for the life he wanted with the woman he loved.

His father's jaw flexed as if he were gritting his teeth. His brocade tunic was rumpled, as though he'd slept in it, and his hair and beard were in disarray. Never in William's life had he seen the laird so unkempt.

"I've failed ye," William said without sorrow. For he did not feel remorse, not when he and his men had tried so hard. Especially not with what he had almost lost.

His father's chin trembled. "My lad." His voice broke, and his gaze turned watery. "My son." He opened his arms and pulled William against his broad chest. "Thanks be to God, ye're safe."

William went still with uncertainty. His father had never embraced him, never shown any sign of affection.

"I thought ye were gone," the old man said. "I thought I lost ye, my son." He leaned back and regarded William with a searching gaze. "Are ye well, lad? Are ye injured?"

William could only stare in reply. This man could not be his father.

"Why do ye suddenly show concern for me?" William asked bitterly. "Did the Campbells offer a wealthy dowry ye couldna turn down?"

His father shook his head. "I've always been concerned about ye. I've always cared."

William pulled his father from the room to the hall, where they were blessedly alone. "Ye stopped caring. I've spent so much of my life hearing what a failure I am. What a disappointment."

Laird MacLeod's shoulders sagged, and wrinkles carved deep lines on his face. "'Tis a woman's role to coddle a child. 'Tis a father's responsibility to ensure his son grows up to be a man. I raised ye as my da raised me. It made ye work harder, be stronger."

William gaped at his father incredulously. "It made me resent ye."

His father winced.

"I dinna want to be laird." A weight lifted from William's chest at his admission. "I dinna want to wed a Campbell lass, or any other than Kinsey."

"The archer?" Laird MacLeod gave a half-grin.

William narrowed his eyes.

"Why do ye no' want to be laird?" his father demanded. "Because ye dinna want to lead yer people or because ye want to marry yer archer?"

"I dinna shy from leading my people," William said with a conviction that resonated in his soul. "But I'll no' put aside love for a union with a woman's dowry."

His father's eyes tensed with a familiar shrewdness. "If ye were allowed to wed her, would ye still want to be laird?"

"Aye."

"An alliance would do well for our clan, but I understand yer decision on marriage." Laird MacLeod tilted his head, his expression almost sheepish. "'Twas one I made myself when I wed yer mum."

William blinked in surprise. "Ye always said her head was in the clouds, and that ye dinna want me to be like her."

His da smiled to himself, as if savoring a private moment of joy. "Aye, she did have her head in the clouds. She was a whimsical lass who dinna take life too seriously and told the most wondrous tales of dragons and brave knights. She would rather have had an armful of flowers than a mountain of gold. The world was a brighter place with her in it." He chuckled at some distant memory. "She'd no' have made a good leader, but she would have been the perfect mother."

Sadness touched his eyes, and he reached out a hand to squeeze William's shoulder. "I'm sorry she dinna get the chance to know ye. She was too damn good for this world, and God knew it."

William swallowed hard at the knot in his throat, at the regret that sat like a rock in his chest. "I dinna know anything about her."

"'Tis my fault." Laird MacLeod sighed and scrubbed the back of his head. "It hurts to speak of her, even now. I think..." His eyes glistened with more emotion than William had ever seen in his father's face. "I think she would be disappointed in how I've raised ye. I dinna let myself consider that until now."

"Will ye tell me about her?" William asked.

Laird MacLeod nodded and gave a hard swallow. "I hope ye can forgive me. That she can, too." He looked upward, as though seeking her approval from the heavens.

His father opened his arms but did not move to William, letting him come of his own volition. William moved forward and embraced his da.

"I love ye, my lad." Laird MacLeod patted William on the back, and they released one another. "And I'd like ye to introduce me properly to yer Kinsey. I have some apologies to make to the woman who will be my new daughter."

His father gave a sheepish grimace, and William couldn't help but scoff. "Aye, that ye do."

Together, they joined the others in the great room. Kinsey met William's eye, her pinched brows expressing her anxiety.

Laird MacLeod went to her first. "I owe ye an apology for many different reasons."

Kinsey tilted her chin higher.

"I'm sorry." He offered her a reverent bow. "I hope ye can forgive me for how I treated ye."

She folded her arms over her chest. "Mayhap ye should consider not making yer son give up his birthright—"

"Nay, he'll still be laird." Laird MacLeod slid his gray eyes to William. "And will wed for love over dowry."

William reached for Kinsey's hand as happy relief eased the tension from her beautiful features.

"Kinsey has a dowry," Drake said.

They all turned to look at him.

"I do?" Kinsey asked.

"Ye're granddaughter to the Ross Chieftain," Drake replied. "Of course ye do."

"The Ross Chieftain?" Laird MacLeod said, his eyes lighting up.

Kinsey scowled. "I want nothing from that bastard." She cast William an apologetic look. "He's a terrible man. I don't want anything to do with him."

"Mayhap ye ought to give him a chance." William glanced at his father. "He might surprise ye."

His da straightened, stony-faced save the twinkle in his eye.

"I can speak with him for ye," Drake said.

Kinsey shook her head. "Nay." She squeezed William's hand. "I can do it myself."

But William knew that before she could seek out her grandfather, she would first have to face her family. Something they would do together.

⚜

THE RIDE TO CASTLETON WAS SHORT AND UNEVENTFUL DESPITE Kinsey's ragged nerves. Several days after they had all reunited at the inn, Laird MacLeod once more assumed control of the army and journeyed to Jedwood Forest to rejoin the king's army, while Drake, William and Kinsey returned to her home. After stopping at Fennela's cottage with her horse and payment, of course.

William and Drake discussed battle strategies most of the way to the manor on the outskirts of Castleton, but Kinsey, who had experienced enough war, was content to be alone with her thoughts.

Her chest still ached from her injuries, and apparently would for at least a fortnight or more, but her head had cleared enough for her to think properly again.

She had much to atone for with her family. Not only for the way she'd left but also for what she'd done to Drake. Her stomach twisted to think of what he'd given up saving not only her, but William and Reid as well. It was a debt she could never repay.

The stone manor came into view, and the talk of battles subsided. William rode to her side and reached a hand toward her. She accepted the gesture of support with a grateful smile.

A face appeared in the open window, and the door flew open as Mum ran out. "Kinsey. Oh, thanks be to God!" Her gaze found Drake. "Ye found her." She looked between them and their battered appearances, her joy melting to shock. "Heavens! What's happened to the lot of ye?"

Clara appeared in the doorway and put her hands over her mouth before joining their mother. "Kinsey, ye're safe."

Kinsey slid from her horse, wincing in pain as she landed. Her mother ran to her, thin hands fluttering as if she wanted to embrace her, but having seen Kinsey's discomfort, was hesitant to do so lest she cause further injury.

"I'm so glad to see ye home," her mother said in a choked voice. "Ye feisty, impulsive lass." The chastisement was light, but Kinsey knew her mother well enough to recognize how badly her heart had been wounded.

"I'm sorry, Mum."

Drake and William dismounted from their steeds as two men emerged from the manor.

Drake's eyes narrowed. "Who are they?"

"Ach, Monroe and Bruce," Kinsey's mother replied with a wave of her hand. "Faye and Ewan sent them down from Sutherland to help look for ye." She smiled back at the two men as they approached. "She's returned."

Kinsey recognized the tall man with his black hair smoothed back in a thong as Monroe, Ewan's advisor, as well as the large man at his side with thick blond hair as one of Ewan's warriors.

Monroe's keen eyes found Kinsey's, and he lowered his head with sincerity. "We're relieved to see ye safely returned."

"They've been looking everywhere for ye," Mum said. "What would possess ye to leave like that?"

As Kinsey considered where even to begin, William cleared his throat and spoke up. "Me."

Mum's attention focused on William, apparently assessing him. "Well, I can see why he won ye over."

Kinsey groaned in humiliation.

William gave her mother his most charming smile. "Aye, by complimenting her archery skills."

"I think there's a lot more to know about this story." Mum wagged her finger at them. "Why dinna ye come inside? Clara, will ye be a dear and fetch us all some ale?"

"Of course, Mum." Clara hugged Drake first, then Kinsey, enveloping her in a sweet, lavender scent, before rushing to see to everyone.

Between Kinsey, William and Drake, the full story came out. Though Kinsey tried to minimize the battle she'd engaged in with Drake, his honesty compelled him to share the extent of what he'd done. He had to pause several times with shame and grief burning in his eyes, especially when their mother began to weep.

It was not the only time their mum cried. When they were finished with the tale, she stared in horror at Drake. "Ye sacrificed yer chance to be a knight to save yer sister." She wiped at the tears in her eyes. "If ever there was a man more chivalrous and deserving of a knighthood..." She shook her head at the shame of the loss. "What of Lord Werrick, will he take ye back as Captain of the Guard?"

"I imagine he would," Drake said. "But I wouldna ask it of him." He squared his jaw. "I couldna sully his home or good name with my disgrace."

"But ye did it to save Kinsey." Clara wiped at her own red-rimmed eyes.

"'Tis why I know he would take me back." Drake's look was set into one of determination, the kind that could never be dissuaded. "And why I'll no' ever ask."

Kinsey's heart crumbled anew in a chest that already burned with each breath. "I cost ye too much."

William gently touched her arm. "'Tis why I've offered the role of Captain of the Guard to him at Dunscaith Castle." He winked at Drake. "I'm only waiting for his reply."

Drake's eyes widened, a tell he immediately corrected. But not before Kinsey caught it, the confirmation that this had clearly not been brought up between them before now.

"My da has seen to the knighting of several men," William continued. "And I know he's verra impressed with ye."

"Oh, Drake." Mum put her hands to her ruddy cheeks, her eyes welling yet again. "Ye can still be a knight. But for Scotland."

"We'd be honored to have ye at Dunscaith," William pressed. "Say aye."

Drake's mouth lifted slightly at the corners, the only amount of pride Kinsey had ever seen him allow himself. "Aye, I'll accept. Thank ye."

"To Drake Fletcher." Monroe, who had been quietly listening in the corner, raised his ale in Drake's direction. "May yer path to knighthood be swift, and yer honor remain true."

They all drank in celebration, the ale sweet and tasting of home in a way that soothed Kinsey's soul.

"Might I ask where ye intend to have the wedding?" Monroe asked.

Kinsey flushed and slid a glance at William. In truth, she hadn't thought of it. She knew only that she had agreed to marry him and would reside with him at Dunscaith while the steward provided him with information on the lairdship and the land, so he would be fully prepared once the honor passed to him someday.

"Dunscaith, I presume," William spoke slowly, studying Kinsey for her reaction. "Or mayhap here?"

"We hadna discussed the details," Kinsey admitted with a laugh.

Monroe smiled kindly. "If I may be so bold, I'd like to suggest Dunrobin Castle. I offer this knowing my chieftain will support the decision. As ye know, Lady Sutherland is with child. I dinna think she could make the journey to either location for many months."

"How very thoughtful of ye." Clara clutched her hands over her chest. "It wouldn't be the same without Faye."

"It would not," Kinsey agreed. "I think Dunrobin sounds perfect."

William took her hand. "Wherever ye are is where I want to be."

Mum gave a wistful sigh, and Kinsey beamed at the man she would soon wed, her heart full. And on their way to Dunrobin, they would stop by Balnagown Castle, for Kinsey to have the second meeting she'd been dreading—the one with her grandda, the Chieftain of the Ross clan.

# EPILOGUE

*January 1342*

*Dunrobin Castle*
*Sutherland, Scotland*

Kinsey's family hadn't been together all at once since they'd tried to save Faye from their grandfather. They were all together now, in celebration of Kinsey's union to William. It wasn't grand, which pleased Kinsey, who had always been more pragmatic than ostentatious. And it wasn't large, being only their families. Which made it entirely perfect.

Kinsey wore a blue silk kirtle with gold thread twinkling through it like stars in an early dawn sky. Though Faye had tried to fuss with her hair to put it up in some billowy bit of veil and twists of netting, Kinsey had insisted on wearing her curls loose.

The way William's eyes lit up when she walked down the aisle told her she'd made the right decision. Once, she'd thought the enraptured way that he'd looked at her was just part of his ploy to lure in women, as much a facade as his charming smile. Now, she knew better.

The Great Hall had been adorned with the finest linen and heaps of food. William and Kinsey were given seats of honor at the front of the dais for all to see and congratulate.

"Thank ye for letting us wed at Dunrobin," Kinsey said to her new husband. "It wouldn't be the same without my family together."

"I meant what I said." He gazed so tenderly at her that she felt a smile stretch over her lips. "I want to be where ye are. That's where I'm happiest." He tilted his head. "Though I'm sure the MacLeod clan will require another celebration when we return home."

*Home.*

It had a lovely ring to it. They had stayed at Dunscaith Castle only a few days before making the journey to Dunrobin, a feat not easily done in the middle of winter. One that was wholly worth it.

"I look forward to it," Kinsey said.

William clinked his cup to hers. "As do I, my love."

*My love.*

How she melted when he used that endearment.

Laird MacLeod approached them after they had all eaten more than they could possibly stand. "Ye've done well in marrying for love, son. 'Tis the greatest path to happiness." He embraced them both. "I love ye, my lad."

"Aye, I know." William smiled at his father in a way that warmed Kinsey's soul. After years of strife between them, they had finally found peace.

"Reid sends his felicitations." Laird MacLeod offered a bow to them both and departed for the evening.

The only way the day could have been any better was if William's oldest friend could have been here with them. Except that Reid was working for the king, who had appropriated Reid's service for his own use. It was indeed a great honor.

Kinsey's family approached. Drake and Mum, Ewan and Faye, of course, and Clara with Faye's wee son, Callum, cradled affectionately in her arms.

Her mother spoke first with tears shimmering in her blue eyes, so like those of her daughters. "Seeing the two of ye wed reminds me of when yer da and I married." She gave a wistful sigh and put her hands over her heart. "I hope ye have the joy we shared for the time we had together, joy like our own Faye found."

Ewan gazed down lovingly at Faye, who leaned tenderly against her husband with a contented smile. "Have ye thought of children yet?"

Kinsey flushed with heat and slid a glance at William, who was usually smooth with answering unexpected questions.

"The first time I realized I wanted to marry Kinsey, I had an image of her holding our child." William put his solid arm around her shoulders. "We havena discussed when, but I'm certain we'll have a bairn or two."

His admission was the first Kinsey had heard of it, and it brought a warmth inside her to know he'd thought of her as a mother. Her cheeks ached from smiling so much, and yet every time she thought to stop, something else would put the grin right back in place again.

"'Tis no' what I heard." Drake crossed his arms over his chest and lifted a brow.

William held up his hands defensively. "I thought ye were going to have her hanged. I was only trying to save my lady love's life." William winked at his new brother. "'Tis a good thing ye were there to help, eh?"

Even Drake had to chuckle at that.

"It gives me such joy to see ye so happy." Clara beamed at them from above a sleeping Callum. There was something so natural in the way she held the bairn, and how sweetly he nuzzled against her, as if she'd been born for motherhood. Clara had never expressed an interest in marriage, or anything for herself for that matter, but Kinsey realized she surely must want something out of life. More than caring for their mother or living in Castleton.

"Mayhap ye'll be next," Kinsey teased.

"If any more of ye get married, I'll no' have any wealth left to give." The Ross Chieftain edged into the group.

Faye narrowed her eyes at their grandfather.

"Dinna look at me like that," he groused. "I dinna have anything to do with this one. But I still took responsibility for my granddaughter."

He reached out and clasped arms with William, his new ally.

Kinsey had dreaded approaching her grandfather, but he'd been surprisingly welcoming to her. Not only had he agreed for the Rosses to become an ally to the MacLeods by virtue of their union, he had also offered her a substantial amount of coin.

It was obvious he was trying to mend the break in their family. Part of her had wanted to trust him, even though a greater part of her still prickled with wariness.

"Ye did," Kinsey agreed. "Thank ye."

The Ross Chieftain grinned at her. "I'm glad ye came to me." He took something from his pocket. "I'm aware no' all of ye are as pleased with my presence, so I'll make this quick and take my leave."

The item in his hand was bound in linen, which he handed to Mum. Drake tensed beside her.

Though her gaze was bright with suspicion, Mum accepted the parcel and slowly began to unroll the linen, revealing what appeared to be a brooch. It was simple but beautiful, with silver filigree framing a delicate golden rose. Kinsey's mother sucked in a sharp breath and snapped her attention to her father.

"What—?" Tears filled her eyes. "How did ye—?"

The Ross Chieftain's jaw tensed. "It wasna my fault." The usual flintiness of his gaze softened. He drew himself ramrod straight, nodded once and left the Great Hall.

Kinsey leaned closer to see the brooch better. "What is it?"

Her mother hastily coiled the linen around the jewelry and folded her hand around it. "'Tis no' anything to concern yerself about."

"He's upset ye." Clara put a hand to their mother's forearm, her brows furrowed with worry.

"I'm fine." Her mother shook her head and hastily swiped at her eyes. "'Tis simply the past and it canna be changed."

But she wasn't fine. That much was as obvious as the understanding that their mother wouldn't speak of whatever it was.

"Ye should wed just to spite him, if nothing else." Faye lifted her brows at Clara with a wicked smirk.

A glint of hurt flashed in Clara's eyes, but she quickly looked down at Callum. "Nay." When she looked up once more, whatever had been there was replaced with her usual happy demeanor. "'Tis the path for ye and Kinsey, but I dinna think it will be for me."

Something in the way she said it twisted hard in Kinsey's chest. Clara had spent far too much of her life sacrificing for everyone else. Drake had been the one to earn money and see them fed after their da's death, but it had been Clara who assumed the responsibility of daily tasks and soothing them all while their mother grieved. It was a duty she'd taken on with her whole heart. One she'd never given up.

But if her heart were so consumed with her family, how could she ever have room for love?

Kinsey resolved then and there to speak to William and Drake later to have Clara and their Mum come live with them at Dunscaith. It might offer Clara a chance to relinquish the responsibility of caring for everyone and make room in her life for the possibility of a future—one just for her.

Love, though unexpected and previously unwanted, had brought light to Kinsey's life she hadn't known possible. One she saw glint in Clara's eyes as she held Callum.

Aye, it was time for Clara to allow herself to be happy on her own. And Kinsey would do everything in her power to make that happen.

After all, she and William had defeated much to get to where they were. Enemies, family struggles, the threat of death and losing one another forever.

Anything was possible.

"What are ye thinking of with that smile on yer lips?" William asked.

She gazed up into his handsome face. "How grateful I am that everything has ended as it has."

"Aye, we've been through a bit. And all worth it." He pressed a kiss to her mouth, sweet and soft. "Ye've made me the happiest man in all of Christendom."

It was true. The struggles had all been worthwhile. For what existed between them was greater than any demons who stood in their path, and their love had truly conquered all.

Thank you for reading KINSEY'S DEFIANCE! I read all of my reviews and would love to know that you enjoyed it, so please do leave a review.

Kinsey's siblings all have their own stories too:

- Faye in *Faye's Sacrifice*
- Clara in *Clara's Vow*
- Drake in Drake's Honor (info coming soon!)
- If you want more stories that take place on the border

between England and Scotland, check out my
Borderland Ladies series and meet Drake, starting with
*Marin's Promise*

CHECK OUT CLARA'S STORY NEXT IN CLARA'S VOW WHERE Clara's intent to join a convent go horribly wrong when she accidentally wounds a Scottish warrior, especially when she realizes he's on an important mission to save thousands of lives.

***Keep reading for a first chapter preview of CLARA'S VOW**

Sign up for my exclusive newsletter to stay up to date on the latest Borderland Rebels news. Sign up today and get a FREE download THE HIGHLANDER'S CHALLENGE.
www.MadelineMartin/newsletter

CLARA'S VOW
Chapter 1 Preview

*March 1342*
*Castleton, Scotland*

Clara Fletcher didn't need anyone to protect her.

If only her family could be convinced.

"The border is dangerous." Drake paced the room, a sign her usually stoic brother was agitated. "With ye both living on Skye, there willna be Englishmen about. Clara willna have to deal with them when she goes to the market. Ye'll no' have to worry about them coming to the manor."

"I can handle myself," Clara said resolutely.

"It isna safe." Drake frowned with concern.

"And bringing her to Skye where there are violent clan wars is any safer?" Mum's fair face flushed. "She's happy here. She's made a life here. Why would ye uproot us like that?"

A coil of frustration tightened in Clara's chest. "I'll be happy anywhere. There's no need to—"

"Clara will have a chance for a better life at Dunscaith." Drake's voice had gone firm.

Mum put her hands on her hips and huffed a sigh. "We have the manor."

"'Tis no' as safe as a castle." A muscle worked in Drake's jaw.

Anger burned in the back of Clara's throat. She hated that everyone saw her as being so helpless, that her future had to be decided for her as if she were incapable of such a feat.

"I can care for myself." She kept her tone neutral so they wouldn't detect her malcontent. "I'm fine here where I can—"

"Ye see?" Mum lifted her chin triumphantly. "She wants to stay. We'll remain here."

A muscle worked in Drake's jaw. "Nay."

"Aye."

Clara gritted her teeth. She wanted to slam her fists onto the scarred wooden table and scream at them both to stop. Her unending patience had hit its ragged bottom, and there was nothing left to scrape up.

She pushed herself up from the bench, strode from the kitchen and climbed the stairs up to her room. No one stopped her. No one so much as bothered to call out to her. This decision was one they intended to make for her as if she were completely inept.

The bedchamber was quiet within, the way it'd been since her younger sister left nearly a year ago. Once, she'd shared the space with both her sisters. It had been filled with chatter and laughter then.

Clara had loved those days.

Her eldest sister, Faye, was forever trying to style Clara's hair a certain way or put her in a new kirtle, having long since given up on doing as much with Kinsey.

There had been disagreements, aye, but there had been quiet

nights where they talked to one another in the darkness. There had been comfort when one of them hurt. There had been love.

Angry voices rose from the kitchen as Drake and Mum continued to argue Clara's fate.

"She canna fend for herself," Drake said.

"She can," Mum shot back. "She just willna do it. She's too good."

Clara's gaze slid to the trunk at the foot of her bed. She kept her daggers inside. A costly set of ten, all polished to a shine and sharpened to a razor's edge. She could defend herself; her mother was correct. After years of practice, Clara could hit the center of the target every time, no matter how far it was placed from her.

If she could see it, she would hit her mark.

But Drake was right too. She couldn't bring herself to harm another person. Was that what made them think her so weak?

If humanity were the essence of being defenseless, then she would accept the harsh judgment. Putting life above emotion took strength—strength she was proud of.

"Ye'd have her closer to yer grandda?" Mum demanded below, the fiery temper she shared with Kinsey breaking through her control.

Clara winced at the reminder of how Faye had been abducted by their grandfather, the Ross clan Chieftain. Aye, her marriage had worked out well, but the unrest between them and the elderly man had been a point of much pain.

There was no good solution. If she chose to remain in Castleton, Drake would worry about them being on the border between England and Scotland. If she chose to go to Dunscaith Castle on the Isle of Skye, where Kinsey lived with her new husband, Mum would be forced to leave the manor she'd worked so hard to make a home.

Clara didn't care where she went. She would find a way to be happy. She always did. Even if the feeling had to be falsified for a while.

She was not happy now. How could she be when the fate of her well-being was tearing her family apart?

Tears welled in her eyes, and she suddenly found herself envious of how Kinsey had decided simply to leave. She'd resolved to go and then did it.

An offer edged into the back of Clara's thoughts. One she'd tucked away and never allowed herself to think of again.

Several months prior, Clara had aided a nun with a cut on her foot. The woman was from a village outside of Glasgow and said they were in sore need of someone with knowledge of healing for their infirmary. Most young women accepted into the convent had a payment to offer, usually a dowry, in exchange for their place among those hallowed walls. But the nun had said Clara's skills were strong enough that such financial considerations could be set aside.

It had been tempting even then, to slip away from the manor, to be one less burden for Drake to care for. She'd stayed for her mother, to help her look after the manor.

Except now she'd become a burden to them both.

Her mother could go to Dunscaith or stay where she was. The choice would be hers to make for herself.

And neither of them need worry after Clara, as she would be in a convent.

The very thought lifted the weight of concern from Clara's chest, and she knew immediately that the decision was right.

Drake and their mother discussed Clara's future late into the night. She'd been half tempted to tell them there was no need, but she knew they would brush off her words.

Instead, she waited until the house went still before slowly, carefully gathering her things. She packed her herbs and healing ointments, some food, a wineskin and cooking pot and a fresh kirtle—more for travel than for her time at the convent, as she knew she would be given a simple tunic like that of the nun she'd helped.

She considered her daggers but left them. She penned a note to her mother, much like Kinsey had. Only this time, Mum need not worry. It wasn't rebels who Clara was joining, but nuns.

What trouble could she possibly find in such a venture?

Before she left the house, however, she returned to her room and lifted the heavy sack of daggers. It wouldn't do to be left unarmed on the road.

With that, she slipped into the stable to pack her horse and then rode out into the dark night, determined to help her family by releasing them of the burden she caused.

REID MACLEOD SHOULD HAVE BEEN ON A SPECIAL MISSION FOR the king rather than carrying a message to Dumbarton. Not that he relished such an honor or was offended that he'd deviated from his purpose. But honor wasn't what Reid wanted out of these raids against the English occupied Scottish territory.

He wanted vengeance.

He wanted to be in the thick of battle, to seek out Lord Rottry and make him pay for what he'd done all those years ago.

Even the thought of the man's name made Reid's blood pulse harder.

Carrying messages was squire's work. However, with so many English about, a warrior needed to be sent, someone who could fight. And these missives were far too important to be diverted. But even knowing the purpose of his role didn't allay Reid's irritation.

He'd been all over Scotland, drenched in its icy late winter rains, slogging through the mud-sucking countryside. First in Aberdeen with the king before being sent down to the Cumberland border. There, they had received word of a massive retaliatory English raid planned on Dumbarton Castle.

Thunder rumbled overhead, like a great beast bearing down on Reid, and the thick cast of clouds blotted out the meager afternoon sun. He hunkered deeper into his cloak and clicked his tongue to hasten his horse.

*More damn rain.*

The impending attack on Dumbarton would happen within a sennight. Not nearly enough time to inform the king and get his men there in time. Thus the Scottish West March Warden had sent his fastest runner to the king in Aberdeen, while Reid was left to inform Dumbarton to prepare for battle. After all, Reid could fight, and the runner could not.

And Dumbarton would need all the warriors it could get.

A scream pierced the air.

Reid straightened in his saddle, immediately on high alert. The wind carrying toward him brought the odor of smoke.

*A fire.*

The woman shrieked again. Reid wasted no time rushing toward the sound. Toward the fire. And, unfortunately, toward the memories.

Thick plumes belched up through the trees. He followed it and came to a clearing where a small hut smoldered. The underside of the thick thatch roof was dry as tinder and now crackled with flame.

Several soldiers stood nearby, a charred torch on the ground at their feet.

Englishmen.

The raw cries of terror came from inside the burning building.

The way it'd been with Reid's mother.

He didn't think anymore after that. There was no logic to his next moves as he flew at the men. There was only the smooth power of his attack, practiced over a lifetime. Death would come to those who tortured and hurt the innocent.

One man fell.

A second.

A third.

The other two attacked, but they were no match for Reid, who swung his great sword with lethal precision. They fell as the door to the small hut flew open, and amid billowing smoke, a woman burst from the doorway. She clutched a boy under the age of five in her arms.

Reid's brother had been that age.

Except it had only been his da—a man whose skills lent themselves to the soil rather than the sword—out there to defend them all.

The woman ran toward him, her face streaked with soot and tears. "Help me."

"Is there anyone else inside?" he asked.

She shook her head, her eyes still wide with horror as she watched her home burn.

An arrow darted out from the surrounding woods and sank in the soil near Reid's feet. He put himself in front of the woman and the boy. "Go to the nearby village." He didn't look back at them to ensure they complied.

Nay, he charged into the woods, determined to kill whoever it was firing arrows in his direction. He saw the bastard between the trees, an Englishman, nocking another arrow.

A stick cracked in the distance. Someone else was nearby.

Reid ignored them and rushed at the archer who fired an arrow in his direction. It sailed past him as two soldiers came at Reid. The archer quickly shot in the direction where the stick had snapped.

Hopefully that meant there would be more Scotsmen for the English whoresons to fight.

Reid dispatched the two soldiers with ease as the archer sent another arrow through the woods. No sooner had Reid's opponents fallen than he was on the archer, jerking his head hard to the right, so his neck gave a sickening crack that reverberated up Reid's palms.

Pressure at Reid's back made him jerk forward, and a burning pain blazed out from the spot. He pitched over the body of the archer with a grunt.

The agony was exquisite and left white-hot stars blinding behind his closed lids.

The gentle shush of footsteps over dry grass pulled his attention momentarily from his agony. Someone was there.

To ensure he was dead?

He was in no condition to fight back, the bastard. He gritted his back teeth.

At least he had saved the woman and her child. He hadn't been able to do the same for his own family. And no one else had been there to do it. Mayhap now, he would join them.

He only wished he'd killed Lord Rottry first.

A delicate lavender scent swept over the odor of blood, followed by the soft intake of breath.

"Ye're not English?" A feminine voice sounded close to Reid's ear, not quite Scottish. But not quite English either.

"Neither are ye," he ground out. The ache of his injury had intensified to the point where even breathing hurt.

"I hit ye." The woman's tone was horrified. "I'm so sorry."

Reid scoffed and pushed himself over to face the woman who had so thoroughly sunk a dagger into his back. But as he looked up, the discomfort in his back faded away, along with the bodies and the blood and the ugly memories dredged up by the burning hut.

He took in the woman's silky dark hair, her pale blue eyes and the sweetness behind them. Her flushed cheeks and earnest expression gave her an innocence that pierced his very soul.

It was *her*.

Kinsey's sister.

*Clara*.

A woman he knew from simply looking at her that he would never deserve. A woman he had wanted since that day he'd caught sight of her at the market.

Now she was here before him. There was so much he ought to say, so much he had imagined. But as he tried to push the thoughts into words in his mind, darkness permeated his head, and everything went black.

## AUTHOR'S NOTE

King David II, only surviving son of Robert the Bruce, had a rather difficult start to his rule. He was an orphan at the age of five and married by the age of seven (his wife, Joan of England was only three - marriages among children were in name and done for political purpose). Two years later, four of his appointed Guardians either died in battle or were taken prisoner. This left his crown vulnerable.

This is when Edward Balliol seized his opportunity and was crowned king of Scotland with the English king's support as well as several Scottish supporters. David and his wife, both under the age of ten, were sent to France for their safety. They would not return again for over seven years.

When they did finally return to Scotland at the age of seventeen, he took control of his country as any teenager could. He charged into battle with the righteous need to reclaim what had been taken from him in his absence. What he couldn't reclaim, he raided.

Raids were awful things. I tried to tame them up as well as I could in Kinsey's story. It was also why I worked so hard to have their characters avoid getting caught up in them.

The purpose of raids was to demoralize and intimidate. Raiding parties could reach up to the thousands and would descend on unsuspecting villages where they would ransack homes, burn cottages, kill and rape villagers and destroy whatever they could.

England was by no means innocent. Both England and Scotland did this to one another through the violent centuries of the medieval ages. England and France also did this against one another through the Hundred Years' War. And on and on, countries around the world did this against one another, as did clans and tribes and communities.

For his part, David's reign was a struggle with much battle and fighting against England, being held captive in England for eleven years before finally agreeing to a ransom he had a hard time keeping up with the payment on and even a divorce from his second wife. However, when he died at the age of 47 (without children), it is said that Scotland was in a place of relative peace and prosper.

# ACKNOWLEDGMENTS

THANK YOU TO my amazing beta readers who helped make this story so much more with their wonderful suggestions: Kacy Stanfield, Janet Barrett and Tracy Emro. You ladies are so amazing and make my books just shine!

Thank you to Erica Monroe with Quillfire Author Services for the consistently amazing edits.

Thank you to Janet Kazmirski for the final read-through you always do for me and for catching all the little last minute tweaks.

Thank you to John and my wonderful minions for all the support they give me.

And a huge thank you so much to my readers for always being so fantastically supportive and eager for my next book.

## ABOUT THE AUTHOR

Madeline Martin is a USA TODAY Bestselling author of Scottish set historical romance novels filled with twists and turns, adventure, steamy romance, empowered heroines and the men who are strong enough to love them.

She lives a glitter-filled life in Jacksonville, Florida with her two daughters (known collectively as the minions) and a man so wonderful he's been dubbed Mr. Awesome. She loves Disney, Nutella, cat videos and goats dressed up in pajamas. She also loves to travel and attributes her love of history to having spent most of her childhood as an Army brat in Germany.

Find out more about Madeline at her website:

http://www.madelinemartin.com

facebook.com/MadelineMartinAuthor
twitter.com/MadelineMMartin
instagram.com/madelinemmartin
bookbub.com/profile/madeline-martin

# ALSO BY MADELINE MARTIN

## BORDERLAND LADIES

*Ena's Surrender (Prequel)*

*Marin's Promise*

*Anice's Bargain*

*Ella's Desire*

*Catriona's Secret*

*Leila's Legacy*

## BORDERLAND REBELS

*Faye's Sacrifice*

*Kinsey's Defiance*

*Clara's Vow*

*Drake's Determination*

## REGENCY NOVELLAS AND NOVELS

*Earl of Benton*

*Earl of Oakhurst*

*Earl of Kendal*

*Discovering the Duke*

*Mesmerizing the Marquis*

## MEDIEVAL NOVELLAS

*The Highlander's Challenge*

*The Highlander's Lady Knight*

*Her Highland Beast*


## HARLEQUIN HISTORICALS

*How to Tempt a Duke*

*How to Start a Scandal*


## HIGHLAND PASSIONS

*A Ghostly Tale of Forbidden Love*

*The Madam's Highlander*

*The Highlander's Untamed Lady*

*Her Highland Destiny*

*Highland Passions Box Set Volume 1*


## HEART OF THE HIGHLANDS

*Deception of a Highlander*

*Possession of a Highlander*

*Enchantment of a Highlander*


## THE MERCENARY MAIDENS

*Highland Spy*

*Highland Ruse*

*Highland Wrath*

Manufactured by Amazon.ca
Bolton, ON

14711777R00143